STAINED

STAINED

JENNIFER RICHARD JACOBSON

A RICHARD JACKSON BOOK
Atheneum Books for Young Readers
New York   London   Toronto   Sydney

Atheneum Books for Young Readers • An imprint of Simon & Schuster
Children's Publishing Division • 1230 Avenue of the Americas, New York, New
York 10020 • This book is a work of fiction. Any references to historical
events, real people, or real locales are used fictitiously. Other names, characters, places, and incidents are products of the author's imagination, and any
resemblance to actual events or locales or persons, living or dead, is entirely
coincidental. • Copyright © 2005 by Jennifer Richard Jacobson • All rights
reserved, including the right of reproduction in whole or in part in any form. •
Book design by Kristin Smith • The text for this book is set in Arrus and
BlurLight. • Manufactured in the United States of America • First Edition •
10 9 8 7 6 5 4 3 2 1 • Library of Congress Cataloging-in-Publication Data •
Jacobson, Jennifer Richard, 1958– • Stained / Jennifer Richard Jacobson.—
1st ed. • p. cm. • "A Richard Jackson book." • Summary: In Weaver Falls,
New Hampshire, in 1975, seventeen-year-old Jocelyn looks for answers
when her lifelong neighbor and friend, Gabe, turns up missing and she
learns that, while her boyfriend has been telling everything to a priest, Gabe
has been keeping terrible secrets. • ISBN 0-689-86745-X • [1. Interpersonal
relations—Fiction. 2. Catholics—Fiction. 3. Priests—Fiction. 4. Child abuse—
Fiction. 5. Homosexuality—Fiction. 6. New Hampshire—History—20th
century—Fiction.] I. Title. • PZ7.J1529St 2005 • [Fic]—dc22 • 2003026670

For Jake, for everything

ACKNOWLEDGMENTS

I am deeply grateful to the following: Franny Billingsley, fellow writer, teacher, and friend, who is the godmother of this book. The High Test Girls, who expressed belief in this novel, nudged periodically, and gave wise and timely advise. The Froggers for their astute insights. Sandy Asher, who pointed out my propensity to view the world in black and white. Toni Buzzeo, Betts Gorsky, and Meg LePage, who were willing to listen to me talk about my characters as if they were real people and helped me to see the story through. Lynn Evarts, Brian Salzar, and readers from DeForest, Wisconsin, for their valuable feedback. Barry Goldblatt, my agent extraordinaire, who accepted me on faith, offered fabulous feedback (on a wacky time schedule), and helped make it happen. My editor, Richard Jackson, for his brilliance, warmth, and ability to ask the right questions at the right moment. And finally, my parents, who have always been there to lend support.

ONE

I'm the first to arrive again. I lock my bike out back and plunk down on the chipped cement steps that lead into the kitchen. Joe's the only one with a key.

I don't mind sitting here. The sun's spreading warmth on my bare legs. I lean back so it can reach my face.

"What are you smiling about?" asks Linda, Joe's wife, as she jumps down from the van. She doesn't expect an answer, and I don't give her one. I follow Joe and Linda into Joe's Grill, punch myself in, and go directly to the coffee station. I try to put my hair up in an elastic, but I'm still holding my dinky white apron, so the attempt is rather sad.

"There's a hairnet in the storeroom," Joe says. I wonder if he's really going to make me wear it this time.

I have no sooner torn open the coffee packet and

poured the contents into a filter when the regulars start to stream in. The Bourgoine family piles into the back booth, and I decide to wait on them before the counter crowd, who are busy dividing the morning paper according to habit.

An hour into my shift I see Benny coming in the door. I take another order—steak and eggs, scrambled eggs and bacon, poached eggs and toast—but my mind is on Benny. Benny pulling me close, close enough to put his hands in my back pockets. I smile and my insides run. Run like the yoke of a soft-boiled egg.

When I turn to place the order, one of the regulars thinks the smile is for him and smiles back.

I walk over to Benny in the corner booth. He has the menu open, but he's not reading it. He's looking out the window instead. Sunlight bounces off his chin-length hair.

"Coffee's ready!" Joe shouts.

I know he hates it when my friends hang out here. I decide to do my waitress act, thinking that might appease Joe and make Benny laugh. "What can I get you, sir?"

Benny raises his eyebrows. The effort almost seems too much. He's not playing along.

So I lower my voice. "You're up early, given how little sleep you got last night." I expect a joke about keeping him up with my talk of weird things, like, what if the whole world is an illusion? What if death is just a skip from one dream into another? At the very least I expect the memory of my touch to move across his face. Nothing.

"I went to Mass this morning, Jocelyn." His tone is serious and cautionary—a tone I respect. I like it that Benny can get heavy from time to time. The wording next to his yearbook picture will not read: *Likes honkin' chicks, stompin' parties, and goin' fast;* it will likely have a quote from Kingsley or Thoreau instead.

"Is your mother okay?"

"She, um, she . . ." He sighs, lowers his head, and pinches the top of his nose. It takes him a moment to regain composure. Then he lifts his head and smiles—the kind of painful smile you offer someone when the only other alternative is crying.

"Well enough to tell me to comb my hair," he jokes.

I place my hand on his arm. "Oh, Benny."

He pulls away. "We've got to talk, Jocelyn. What time do you get off today?"

"Four. I'll get you juice and an omelet." I move away quickly, and as I'm handing the order to Joe, I let Benny's abrupt manner play in my brain. He didn't go to Mass just to pray for his sick mother, he went because of me.

I place a knife down in front of him. "You talked to Father Warren this morning, didn't you?"

Benny just nods. His dark eyes lock onto mine. Sometimes I feel like the only place I exist is in those eyes. "Let's talk about it, Jocelyn," he says in a loud whisper. "I can't help what I believe."

"I gotta work." I take my order pad and greet the couple at the next table. He knows that I know he's breaking up with me.

"I'll meet you outside at four," he says, leaving before his food arrives.

I can't think. The Grill starts to fill up. I take an order and put the slip in my pocket. I don't remember it until I hear a woman say, "I could have served the whole place French toast by now." I clip the order to the wheel, but I'm too shaky to ask Joe to rush it.

I hand a man some salt, and he says, "This don't look like the pepper I asked for, sweetie." Damn Benny.

If Gabe were here, I could duck out long enough to swear, to cry, to pull myself together. I grab a bucket and begin clearing syrupy plates off a table. I toss the plates, coffee mugs, silverware, and juice glasses in with as much clatter as I can make. When Joe turns around to see what's going on, I glance up at the clock.

Joe knows that Gabe will never make it in at seven on a Saturday morning, so he gives him a later punch-in time. Then Gabe's late only half as often.

Today Gabe doesn't show up at all. Joe calls his house and talks to Margo, Gabe's mother. Joe sounds friendly, a little concerned, like he might have gotten Gabe's schedule mixed up, like Joe could be at fault. But that tone is for Gabe's parents. Here at the Grill, Joe is seething. He feels betrayed. He can't wait until Gabe walks in the door. He's gonna pop his head off.

The angrier Joe gets at Gabe, the better I look. Mistakes are forgiven. I set places, suggest Joe's homemade hash, clear plates on route to picking up orders. Looks like I'm on an even keel. Only I know better.

T W O

We are four years old. Our mothers are having coffee and smoking cigarettes on the back deck. Gabe's mother doesn't have a cigarette in her hand. She says that Mike would kill her before the cigarettes do. Mike is her husband and Gabe's daddy. But she takes the cigarette out of my mother's fingers and sucks on it when she thinks Gabe and I aren't watching. My mother is divorced and doesn't care what Mike or anyone else thinks about smoking.

Gabe and I put our feet on the bottom rail and look out at the river that flows by our side-by-side backyards. Gabe steps up to the middle rail and leans over. I do the same, careful to keep my bum in the air so I don't topple headfirst onto the lawn that rolls down to the sudsy water.

"Get down from there, you two," my mother says.

"Go wash that grime off your hands and I'll give you cookies."

I go into the bathroom, pull down my shorts, and scootch up onto the toilet. Gabe follows me in and begins to wash his hands. He makes a big ball of foam with the soap and then wipes it on a towel. He looks at me looking at him. Then he shuts the bathroom door from the inside and slides down in front of it. He puts his arms around his folded knees and bends his head. I can see the blond stripes on top. I'm counting them when he lifts his head back up.

"You can't get out," he says.

I don't say anything.

"You can't get out, you know."

I don't know this game. I don't know what I'm supposed to do. I slide off the toilet and pull up my shorts.

"I can see your underpants," he says.

I tuck in the elastic so he can't see any part of them.

He tries again. "You can't get out."

"I can too," I say. I try to take his arm to pull him away from the door. But he has one hand locked around the other wrist, and I can't pull them apart. His sneakers stick to the linoleum floor. He doesn't budge, but his eyes do a little sparkle dance.

Sometimes I like it when his eyes smile.

Sometimes they scare me. I back up and look out the window screen.

Gabe gets up to see if I can escape this way. I try to run to the door.

He runs back and stands in front of it.

"You can't get out."

I think of yelling, but I don't.

I never do.

He's right. I can't get out. I sit down on the floor. I wonder how long someone can stay in a bathroom. After a few more moments I lean my face against the cold porcelain of the toilet bowl. I wait.

Eventually, Gabe gets bored and leaves.

I can't believe that I'm free. So I just sit a while longer. Finally, I get brave. I leave the bathroom and get a vanilla wafer. The mothers don't talk to me. They don't know I was missing.

I go outside and look for Gabe. A fisherman's dog tries to get my cookie. I hold it in the air. Gabe comes barreling out of nowhere. He knocks me down and sits on my stomach. He pins my hands up by my head.

I don't mind it so much when Gabe traps me this way. Maybe my eyes smile too.

THREE

It's 3:52. Joe sees Benny waiting on the front steps of the Grill.

"Get out of here," Joe says to me. Benny's making him nervous.

I take my apron off, fold it into a square, and put it in my pocket. I open the door and stand on the top step.

"Come on," Benny says. He walks to the back of the Grill, where there's a trash house and a few crummy picnic tables. I follow, dragging my feet. The very first time Benny came by to pick me up at the Grill, he stepped down from the steps, stopped, and stared at me. He just stared and smiled.

"What?" I asked. "What is it?"

"You."

That's all he said. "You." Like that was all he ever asked for—all he ever needed.

Now Benny sits on a table that has a broken leg. The table wobbles. Flies hover.

"Let's go down to the river," I suggest. I want to take his hand and pull him down the bank, through the tall grass. I want to sit underneath the rushing falls.

"I can't, Jocelyn," he says.

"Why not?" My voice is that of Evil Soap Opera Girl. Evil Girl pretends to be sweet and innocent while deviously luring Boy away from goodness. Viewers know that Evil Girl is a manipulative bitch. But Boy doesn't figure it out. He wants to be lured.

Not Benny, though. Not this time.

"You know what will happen if we go down to the river."

I know. I know that if I draw lines on Benny's fingers or pictures on his strong forearms, he'll sigh. And he'll pull me close, and he'll listen, or at least pretend to listen to *my* reasoning about love while his fingers find the softer parts of my body. I will tell him that wanting to touch each other is instinctive, that we are only expressing our God-given feelings.

But, Benny will say, *the Church says it's wrong. Father Warren says it's wrong. I gotta listen to what The Man says.* He'll raise his eyes toward heaven as if I have just slithered up from the bowels of the earth and have no idea who "The Man" is.

Truth is, I don't know if what Benny and I do is wrong. I just know that it makes me feel wanted. Like someone is so very pleased that I am here on this earth.

"I made a deal, Jocelyn." Benny's voice is far away. Another town. Another universe. He fingers the silver Saint Christopher's medal around his neck, a medal for protection. Protection from me. "In church this morning I made a deal."

"For your mother?" I ask. But I already know the answer. Benny swapped being with me for his mother's life.

Benny nods. "You know I want to be with you, Joss. I think you're fantastic. You—God, this is so hard."

"Then don't do it, Benny. Don't do this to us."

"I have no choice, Joss." Benny puts his elbows on his knees and his head in his hands.

And I have no answers. We tried being "just friends," but it didn't keep. One of us makes a move toward the other, and it's all over. I turn and head home.

"Jocelyn. Come back!"

Benny follows for a ways. I know that he wants this to end well. I can feel him stop and stand in one place, hoping I'll turn around so he can do something magnanimous, like kissing me on the forehead. Or touching me on the cheek. Somebody taught him sweet. I want to stop, I really do, but I can't bear to have him tell me good-bye. I don't look back. I keep walking. It isn't until the big white town houses with porch swings turn to cabins with multiple additions and hanging tires and the sidewalks bleed into gravel that I buckle over and gasp for air.

I am playing church in my backyard. I have all my dolls lined up on a picnic bench. The parted mouths of the dolls, fitted for baby bottles, have Necco wafers stuffed inside. I place a white one in my mouth. It feels silky and hot at the same time. In a moment I will dribble water, colored with red food coloring, down my dolls' fronts. I have never taken Communion, but I know that it means that baby Jesus belongs to you and that seems like a very lucky and special thing.

Gabe, his brothers Matthew and Timmy, and his father are trying to fix their dock. So far it is a five-swear job. All of the swears have come from Mike. If one of the boys said a swear, Mike would cuff him.

"Matthew, get me a Phillips screwdriver," he yells.

Matthew brings him a screwdriver.

"I said a Phillips! That's not a Phillips! Haven't

I taught you anything? God, not one of you has an ounce between the ears!"

Matthew looks at Timmy and makes his eyes roll back. Gabe goes over to the tool bag and pulls out the right screwdriver. But when he reaches his father's outstretched hand, he doesn't hand it over. "Let me screw it in," he says.

"When you're older," says Mike. "Give it here."

Gabe doesn't budge. "I can do it," he says.

Church is over. I'm clutching my favorite doll— and my breath.

"Gabe!" Mike yells. But then he backs up and says, "Okay, wise guy. You think you're so big. Screw it in. Go ahead. Do it!"

Gabe takes the screwdriver and places it into the top of the screw. He starts to turn it, but the screwdriver slips out. He tries again.

"You're such a man, Gabe," says Matthew. Gabe's brothers and his father laugh. Then they turn away.

Gabe stays. He locks his jaw and pushes down on the screw. Something budges. Little by little, he makes the screw turn. It digs into the wood.

"Hey, Dad!" he yells. "Hey, Dad! I'm doing it!" But Gabe's daddy is working at the end of the dock and pretends not to hear.

Gabe throws the screwdriver down and starts marching up to the house.

His father tells Timmy about the last time he had to fix this "gaawram" dock.

"Gabe," I call out. "Come see what I'm doing."

Gabe keeps walking. He's going to slam a door, I think. But then he changes his mind and comes over.

"I've never had a brown one," Gabe says, pulling a wafer out of a Chatty Cathy's mouth.

I know he's lying. And I know he'll eat every single one of my Necco wafers if I let him. I do.

As I approach our A-frame house I hear my mother talking inside. Her women's group? I try to walk directly upstairs to my room, but she calls me through to the front room.

"Just a minute," I say, and duck into the bathroom to look in the mirror. My eyes are red but not puffy. I can tell them it's the smoke from the Grill if they ask. But they don't, and I immediately see why.

Margo, Gabe's mother, is sitting at the kitchen table, crying. Mike is sitting across from her. My mother is standing behind her, her hands on Margo's shoulders.

"Gabe didn't come home last night," my mother says. Her statement is part declaration, part question.

"He wasn't at Joe's today either." I figure they already know this, but I don't know what else to say.

My mother tells me with her eyes to sit down.

"Jocelyn, do you know anything about Gabe that might give us a clue to his whereabouts?"

"We've called his friends, Jocelyn," Margo explains. "And everyone on the baseball team. None of them have seen him since the party last night. Did you see him there?"

"Was he drinking?" asks Mom.

What do I do? I look at Mike just sitting there playing with the salt and pepper shakers. He doesn't look up. Do I say, *Yes, he was three sheets to the wind?* "It was an end-of-the-year party," I say instead. In other words, *You connect the dots.*

"Was he with anyone special?" asks Margo.

"Bernadette?" asks Mom.

"I didn't see Bernadette at the party," I say.

"Well, that's a relief." Margo puts her tissue down and picks up her coffee mug. Her hands are shaking.

"Perhaps he left the party to go to Bernadette's," Mom suggests lightly. We both know that this is Margo's worst fear.

Mike gets up and looks out the sliding door. "When I get my hands on that kid . . ."

I look at Mom. What's going on?

The O'Neils have called the police, Mom tells me. They've called the church, too. Gabe is missing. In two more hours they will start an official search. "Jocelyn, can you think of anything that could help?

Do you know anything about Gabe that Margo and Mike might not know?"

"Has there been any trouble?" his mother asks. "Drugs?" She is begging me to tell her anything, no matter how heartbreaking.

Until now the two families have pretended that Gabe and I are in the same league. That we're both having the time of our lives during these exciting high school years. But we all know that Gabe is a golden boy, an all-star, and that I am barely making it as fringe. If it weren't for Benny, who moved into town in January, and Theresa, who has remained my best friend since we discovered that we both loved *Wuthering Heights* at the end of seventh grade, I would be a total outcast. Gabe and his friends couldn't possibly tell anyone in the room whether or not *I* was at the party last night.

Until today Gabe could do no wrong. They're asking me to share the perceptions of an observer, a loner—not an insider. Their eyes plead for information.

"I don't know of any trouble," I say. "But I'll see what I can find out."

They nod in relief. It's funny, but for a moment I feel that invisible chord that used to bind Gabe and me. Maybe I can help.

Gabe and I have started Mrs. Story's kindergarten, but it's Friday night and we're allowed to stay outside until our mothers have finished their martinis and eaten all of the baby cocktail franks out of the fondue pot. Gabe's oldest brother, Matthew, and his sister, Mary, are at parties. His middle brother, Timmy, and his dad are at their house watching *77 Sunset Strip* on television. I can see flashing blue images through the windows. Gabe and I are sitting at the picnic table on my back deck staring at our ham and cheese sandwiches. Our mothers have said that we can't get up from the table until they are finished. I hate ham. Gabe hates soggy cheese.

He yells that we are getting eaten alive by mosquitoes. My mother stomps out on the deck, lights a stinky candle in a peanut butter jar, and places it in the middle of the table. "There. That will keep the bugs away. Eat your dinner."

Despite its smell, the candle seems to be having little effect on the bugs. The mosquitoes are still humming, and within seconds, moths have the candle surrounded. Little white moths and larger gray moths with furry bellies flit in and out of the jar. We hear a fast sizzle now and then—a moth flying too close. Gabe takes a stick and tries to poke them farther into the fire.

"Cut it out, Gabe," I say. I hate the thought of singed moths.

He won't stop.

I blow out the candle.

"Mom!" Gabe yells.

In the faint porch light I can see that there are moths that have flown too close or have stuck to the melted wax. "Let's give these poor moths a funeral," I suggest—partly because I feel bad for the moths, partly because I want to stop Gabe from telling on me.

Gabe looks inside the jar. "We can't," he says matter-of-factly.

"We could bury our sandwiches at the same time," I suggest, thinking that our table sentence is the obstacle.

"No," says Gabe. "They can't have a funeral 'cause they did suicide."

I have no idea what Gabe is talking about. He can tell because my mouth is shut.

"Suicide is when someone kills themself."

"Why would someone do *that*?" How is such a thing possible?

"Lots of people do," Gabe says. He begins whipping the bread from his sandwich into the woods. "They blow their brains out. Or they jump in front of the train. Matthew told me."

I remember hearing that someone had died in a train crash last year, but I thought it was an accident. I thought they had been too pokey in getting over the tracks. I try to imagine someone wanting to die.

"Do they want to go to heaven? Is that why they do it?"

"They can't!" Gabe is getting impatient with my lack of knowledge. "If you kill yourself, you're a sinner. They're sinners, so they can't have a funeral and they have to go to hell."

"Hell?" I whisper so our mothers won't hear me say a swear word. "Hell with the devil?"

"Of course! Don't you know anything?" Gabe's sandwich has vanished. Mine still sits in front of me.

What were those moths thinking of, I wondered, when they flew so close to the flame?

SEVEN

I change out of my uniform, put on my favorite pair of bell-bottoms. I let my hair out of the elastic and shake my head. Wild hair. Theresa picks me up in her orange Bug. We're going to Katherine LeBlanc's party. I wasn't planning to go—it seemed wrong with Gabe missing—but I had promised to find out what I could, and a party was a good place to start. I certainly wasn't going to learn anything sitting around at home. I made Mom promise to call the LeBlancs if Gabe was found.

Theresa's wearing a short peasant dress and sandals. She is practically sitting on her long straight hair. She will be the only one wearing a dress tonight, but everyone's used to her having her own style. I stare at her, and then I try to remember my own image in the bathroom mirror. I can't. Already, I'm fading away. Our favorite song, "You Sexy Thing," comes on the radio. Normally, I would crank it, and Theresa and I would sing at the top of our lungs. But tonight we're distracted.

Theresa and I talk about Gabe. I think he's been kidnapped like Patty Hearst. He'll be brainwashed into robbing banks and acting as a terrorist. Or, worse, he'll be forced into a life of prostitution.

"Well, he does have the bod," says Theresa. "He'd make big bucks."

I give her a look that says, *Oh, that's sympathetic.*

"But you know where I think he is?" She doesn't wait for me to answer. "I think Bernadette's pregnant. I bet Gabe drove her down to Boston last night. Maybe she scheduled an abortion for today. Maybe something happened. Maybe she chickened out and Gabe's still with her. That's what happened to Sue Hopkins."

Theresa had told me about Sue. They're in drama club together. Kids consider Theresa knowledgeable, a little worldly. That's why they're always confiding in her. Sue probably figured that she would tell me, but that didn't concern her. Where could it go next?

I think about Sue and her boyfriend riding the subway all night long. It makes me feel so sad. "Benny broke up with me today."

Theresa pulls over to the side of the road. She bangs the horn. "Again? He is so cruel. What is it with you and cruel guys, Jocelyn?" She hugs me over the stick shift, and I wonder what she means. For years I wouldn't even try to talk to a guy. I have only had one boyfriend. I have only had Benny.

I wait for her to ask me why: *Why did he break up with you?* I want to explain. I want to say that Benny's scared. But Theresa doesn't ask why we broke up. It's as if she knew it was coming, the way she knew that the sun would rise today. It was simply a matter of time.

Mrs. Cavanaugh is watching me and Gabe. My mother is at school learning to be a counselor. Gabe's mother is doing her volunteer work at church. Mrs. Cavanaugh gives us Pop-Tarts and tells us to eat them outside. Strawberry Pop-Tarts. "But don't go into the garden," she says—just like Mrs. Rabbit. And just like Peter, that's where we head first.

Gabe is standing on a daffodil.

"Stop killing it," I say.

He moves off it. Then he picks it. "Hey," he says, "let's pick a whole bunch of these!"

"Mrs. Cavanaugh said not to go in the garden."

"Let's pick bunches of flowers and sell them," says Gabe.

"Why?" I ask.

"For money."

"Who will get the money?" So far any money I had went into the collection basket at church.

"We will, stupid. We'll buy candy."

"We can sell the flowers on Pine Street and then go to Ray's Market."

Mrs. Cavanaugh will be furious if she sees that we've picked her daffodils and early lilies. She'll scold us until we pretend to cry if she finds out that we've walked to Ray's. But I know that Ray's has wax lips. And I have always wanted wax lips.

Gabe and I try to pick only the flowers that are in the middle of leaves so Mrs. Cavanaugh can't tell. But I keep seeing that Gabe has more than me, and he keeps seeing that I have more than him, so we keep picking until our own bunches get bigger and bigger.

Then we knock on doors.

There is no one home at the first house.

At the second house a mother in curlers comes to the door. She thinks we look cute. We tell her that a bunch of flowers costs ten cents. She buys a bunch of flowers from each of us. I don't know how many flowers to give her, so I watch Gabe. He gives her four, so I give her four. She gives us each a dime.

We walk up the path of the next house. There are daffodils and crocuses all along the walkway. *Whoever lives here likes flowers,* I think. We're gonna be rich.

We knock on the door. A dog barks.

"Nobody's home," Gabe says.

"Yes, there is," I say. I can hear someone telling the dog to stop barking. "Knock louder."

Gabe and I both knock on the door at the same time. I put one hand around my eyes and look through the skinny window next to the door. There is a diamond pattern in the glass. I see an old woman. She sees me and walks down her front hall.

She opens the front door, and before Gabe has a chance to ask her if she wants to buy flowers, she screams.

"You picked my flowers! Get out of here. Shoo! I didn't want my flowers picked. Get out of here!"

I have never seen an old woman holler. Her mouth grows large, and her crooked teeth stick out at me. I drop my flowers on the step and run to the end of the walkway.

"They're not your flowers. We didn't pick your ugly old flowers!" Gabe shouts at her.

"Go. Go now or I'll call the police," she threatens him, using her finger.

Gabe turns and walks toward me. The woman shuts her door. Gabe picks up a rock that edges her pretty path and hurls it toward the skinny window.

We run down Pine Street so fast, I can't feel my legs. I hear the crash over and over in my mind. I picture diamonds raining all over her front steps.

We see a black car at the stop sign ahead. "Come

on," says Gabe, and he pulls me into some scratchy bushes. I stare at the baby leaves on the bushes and try to stop shaking. The car passes. It's a police car.

I start to cry. Gabe wraps his arms around me. "Don't cry, Jocelyn. We didn't pick her flowers. Besides," he says, not worried at all, "my daddy's strong. He won't let them put us in jail."

That night my window is open. I hear the O'Neils' phone ring. I hear Gabe's daddy take him outside. "What were you thinking?" he shouts. "How do you think that behavior reflects on us? You do something like that again and you can pack your bags."

I picture Gabe walking away with all his toys in crumpled paper bags. I close my eyes when I hear the belt. *Cry, Gabe,* I think. *Please cry.*

But he doesn't.

I see him. We've no sooner gotten out of the car when I see Benny walking into the house with Mark Shaw, an all-star baseball player. Unlike last night's party, this is an invitation-only affair. Theresa and I got invitations because we completed Katherine's yearbook assignment. Last I knew, Benny didn't have an invitation. My stomach lurches somewhere between hope and nausea. What has changed?

No one greets us at the door. There are no records playing. No giddy voices made high from pot smoked in the backyard. Then I see why. Officer Beauchamp, affectionately known as Champy, and another cop are at this party. They're looking for information. They're looking for Gabe.

Theresa and I move toward the side of the room. I take a chip from a bowl on the baby grand and plunge it into some onion dip. It takes everything I have to keep from looking at Benny.

Katherine and her friends hold Pepsi bottles like microphones and talk to the jocks who are waiting to talk to the police along the sliding glass windows at the back of the room. Behind them is this amazing view of the mountains.

Father Warren arrives. Katherine's parents, who would normally have removed themselves to the upstairs bedroom, feel the need to stay and chaperone. They move toward Father Warren to welcome him. He is an older priest, but not too old. His hair has just begun to turn white, and he looks kind of cool in his black clothes.

He walks toward Theresa, and I get ready to back away.

"Hello, Jocelyn," he says before I have the chance. I'm surprised that he knows my name. I smile a goofy smile and say nothing. He reminds Theresa that the parish house is always open and that if we're troubled by Gabe's disappearance, it's a place to come, a place to talk. I stare at his hands while he's talking. They are long and freckled and kind, I think.

He turns and talks with the police and then moves to the back of the room to join the players. They open the circle to welcome him. Although he's been in town a year and a half, Father Warren has retained the popularity of a new boy. Mr. LeBlanc leans over the crowd to hand Father a beer, something he would have done for everyone if the police hadn't showed up at the party too.

Benny is on the edge of their circle. I'm about four circles away. I use my peripheral vision to watch him.

Father Warren pulls Benny into the jock crowd and introduces him to a graduate. I can tell that Benny says hi in that smooth way of his—friendly, but with something held back. Like everyone in the room, Father Warren is appropriately somber and concerned, but he bends a little closer to the guys to talk privately. He rests one of those kindly hands on Benny's shoulder. I predict a priest joke. Sure enough, the group chuckles loudly enough to startle one of the cops.

Benny's eyes shift with the laughter. He looks right at me. He raises his hand in a sort of half wave, but he frowns a little.

I try to look indifferent, but my heart is begging a ride. Benny mouths words to me. I don't understand what he's saying. I tell myself to go over and talk to him, but I can't. We both know that between the jocks and me looms a line that I, Miss Doesn't Rate, can't cross.

Father Warren glances over at me, smiles an all-knowing smile, and then pulls Benny back into the discussion.

T E N

I'm sitting at the table trying to stay within the lines of a picture in a coloring book when Margo, carrying a big shopping bag, pushes open the front door. Gabe comes running past her.

"Let's go catch frogs," he says.

"Not so fast, honey," says Margo. She plops her bag down on the couch and says, "Come see what I have for you, Jocelyn."

"Well, good morning to you, too," my mother says to Margo.

I come closer, and Margo pulls a poofy white dress from the bag. At first I think it's a party dress, but then I see the hat and I know it's for a bride.

"This was Mary's First Communion dress," Margo says. "I thought you might like to wear it when you make your First Communion."

She holds the dress up to me. White showers me from shoulders to toes.

"You know that I was going to ask you to stand in for Jocelyn's godmother," my mother says.

"Of course you were," says Margo. "Who else would you ask?" Both my mother and Margo laugh.

I can't believe it! Margo is my fairy godmother, and she's going to make me beautiful, just like Cinderella's godmother made Cinderella beautiful.

Margo says, "I have something else for you." She lifts a little blue and white box out of the bag.

Gabe comes running over to see what other gifts his mother is bestowing on me.

Inside the box is a gold cross hanging from a fragile, gold chain.

"Oh," says my mother.

"I want a cross," says Gabe.

"This cross is for Jocelyn," says Margo.

"Why?" asks Gabe. "You're *my* mother. How come you're giving the cross to Jocelyn?"

"This is a girl's cross," replies my mother in a voice that says, *That should settle it.* But it doesn't.

"Boys wear crosses too," Gabe says to Margo. "Just like this cross. Plain gold."

"That's true," says Margo, holding the chain closer to her eyes, and for a moment I believe she is going to change her mind. But instead, she undoes the clasp and says, "Come here, Jocelyn." She spins me around and clasps the cross around my neck.

"That's sweet of you," my mother says.

"She's a sweet girl," says Margo.

"When she's sleeping."

I thank Margo and follow Gabe outside to catch frogs.

Once we're out on the back deck, though, Gabe seems to forget all about the frogs.

"I really like that cross, Jocelyn," he says to me.

"Me too," I say.

"Boys can wear crosses, you know."

"I know."

He reaches over and lifts the cross from my chest. I feel the chain tighten on my neck as he brings it closer to his eyes.

Please don't break it, I whisper in my head.

Gabe throws the chain back at me and runs down to the river.

God heard me.

ELEVEN

"Did you notice?" Theresa has been talking to me, but I haven't been listening. She's made a potato chip and dip sandwich.

"Notice what?"

"Bernadette's not here. I bet my theory's right."

"Bernadette is never around when Gabe's not," I say. Bernadette doesn't go to Weaver Falls High. She lives in the next town over. She sometimes wanders into the Grill on Saturdays or attends school events when Gabe is playing or has his arm around her, but she never seems to speak to the other kids who trail Gabe for excitement. I wonder how he met her.

"No one else takes her seriously," Theresa says.

"What do you mean?"

Theresa looks at me as if I have two heads. "Gabe dates her for one thing, Joss."

This has never occurred to me before. I try to adjust my picture of the two of them, as if trying to bring a TV screen into better focus. Sure, Bernadette does dress in kind of a slinky way, but does this limit their relationship to sex?

"Theresa!" It's Joanne Montgomery. The first thing you think about when you see her is *The Unsinkable Molly Brown.* She played the title part in last year's musical.

"Hey, Ms. Molly," Theresa says.

"Hi, Joanne," I say.

"Isn't this weird, Theresa, about Gabe O'Neil?" Joanne says. "I just heard the police telling Father Warren that none of his clothes or his extra cash was missing."

I wonder if anyone could tell if Gabe packed just a few things—say, in an overnight bag—and I'm about to ask this, but Joanne is filling Theresa in on the last conversation she had with Gabe. It sounds as if it was a while ago and rather meaningless, but for some reason, Joanne thinks it's significant.

I retreat and walk out the side door, onto the back lawn. Normally, there would be lots of kids out here. No doubt the LeBlancs thought that this is where the party would happen. It's warm, and there are lawn chairs and card tables scattered about.

Okay, so I kind of hope Benny will turn around

and see me here. Maybe he'll come out, where we can talk alone.

I stare at the mountains and think about Gabe. I remember a Saturday a couple of months ago when we were working together. It was late afternoon, and Joe had gone to a chamber of commerce meeting. "I trust you guys to hold the fort," he said.

First Gabe made himself a double chocolate shake. Then he went down to Ray's Market and returned with two scratch-and-win tickets. He sat up on the counter, two tickets in hand, and kicked his feet while I waited on a couple of young girls who came into Joe's for Cokes.

"Which ticket do you want, Joss?" Gabe asked.

"They're your tickets," I said.

"How about this," he said, waving a ticket. "I bet that this here ticket is a winner. If I'm right, I get to keep both tickets. If I'm wrong, you get the other ticket."

I shrugged. Why was he including me?

He pulled a dime out of his pocket and rubbed the silver off the game circles. For a moment his eyes lit up. Then they dropped. "Yours," he said, and handed me the other ticket.

I started to scrape mine. Gabe pulled me closer so he could look over my shoulder. I felt his hands resting on my shoulders, and I could hardly scrape it.

But then the bell over the door jangled, and Bernadette walked in.

"Hey, Bernie," Gabe said, jumping off the counter. "Do you know Jocelyn?"

Bernadette and I both offered quick and awkward hi's.

Gabe slid sideways into a booth—one knee propped up on the seat. Bernadette joined him on the opposite seat. As I washed the tables down I couldn't help glancing over. There was something that distinguished Bernadette from other high school kids. She seemed so sophisticated, so aware in this kind of voluptuous way. I felt like an immature, giddy two-year-old when she was around.

They chatted across the table in low voices. A few stragglers had begun coming into the Grill, so I caught only a word here and there. Words about a prom dress that Bernadette had seen in a window (had Gabe asked her yet?) and about a double play that Gabe described in detail—most likely an instant replay of last night's game. Then Bernadette left. Gabe puttered around out back for a while. When I started to wash some soaking pots and pans, he joined me at the sink.

"So what'd you win?" he asked.

"Nothing. It was a dud."

Gabe made a pouting face.

I started to walk into the back room and then thought to say, "I assumed you'd want me to cover for you—to punch you out." It was almost closing time. If Joe weren't back by then, I'd close up the Grill. I'd covered for Gabe before.

"Bernadette probably thought the same thing," Gabe said.

I looked at his eyes to get his meaning.

"I like to keep her guessing."

"You do?" This question spilled out of me. They looked so honest together. That Gabe would play games with her like this . . . well, that was hard to believe.

He smiled. "Yeah. Sometimes when I'm with her, I won't even touch her. Not once."

That would drive me out of my skin. I wouldn't be able to stand it if Benny and I were together and he didn't take my hand or comb his fingers through my hair or something.

The thought of Benny and I never touching again catapults me back to reality, back to remembering that Benny and I are no longer, period. I get up and head back inside. I gotta get Benny to talk to me. I gotta know what he was trying to say.

A cop stops me as I pass. He basically asks me the same questions my mother and the O'Neils asked me. Only first he wants to know my relationship to Gabe.

I tell him that we are neighbors, that we both work at Joe's Grill on Saturdays and during summer vacation.

"Is that it?" he barks at the end of our brief conversation.

For a moment I think to tell him that we used to take baths together. "That's it," I say instead.

I feel a flood of departures around me. Most of the jocks are bored and leaving for places unknown. Benny's gone.

Theresa offers to cruise, but I can tell that she's not up for a night of driving, so I have her take me home. Mom isn't here—probably with the O'Neils. I walk over to the phone on the kitchen wall and dial Benny's number. I hear a male voice say, "Hello?" But it's Benny's father, not Benny. I hang up.

Upstairs in my room under the eaves I open the pine box my father made me when he was a senior in high school. Inside is a picture of my dad and me when I was three. He's holding me on his lap, and I'm running my hand over his scruffy chin. I don't really remember this moment. All that I remember is this: wrapping my arms around his forehead while he carried me on his shoulders; playing a game where I approached him while he was watching TV and he trapped me in his legs; his going out the door with his knapsack and his car keys while my mother screamed, "Don't go!"

That was the last time I saw or heard from him. For a while people told my mom where my dad was staying, but eventually, everyone in Weaver Falls lost interest.

Also in the box is an ID bracelet that Benny gave me for my seventeenth birthday. On the back he had engraved the year, 1975, and our initials. It's hard to believe that he gave this to me only a month ago. I keep it in the box for fear of losing it.

Under the ID bracelet are two tickets. One is the worthless lottery ticket that I had rubbed thin at Joe's; the other is Gabe's ticket that he'd left on the table when we closed that evening. For some foolish reason, I had reached down and grabbed it. He had won ten dollars. I still don't know what that means. Nothing makes sense. Nothing. A tear rolls down my face, and I stick my tongue out to catch it.

TWELVE

I am in Sunday school. Sister Louise is preparing us for our First Communion. I picture myself in the white dress that's hanging in my closet, the one that Margo gave me. In my picture I'm kneeling and my hands are folded, just like Saint Imelda in the engraving that Sister showed us. Even God is proud.

The boys aren't listening. They shout and tease one another. One boy takes another's Jesus coloring book. A bossy girl tells him to give it back. The boys laugh. They chase.

Sister Louise shouts at the class. She tells the boys to sit down. "You will have to confess your sins to the priest!"

This gets everyone's attention. *Now?* we wonder.

"Before you make your First Communion," says Sister Louise, softly, like she's telling a secret. "Before you make your First Communion, you will have to confess your sins."

"Why?" asks one of the bad boys.

"Your souls are stained. Dirty as coal. If you could look inside yourself, you'd see. They are not made pure until you confess your sins and take your First Communion."

"That's why some children can't go to heaven," says a knowing girl. "Their souls aren't clean. They have to float in purgatory."

I am not sure how the rules work. Does everyone in the class have a stained soul or just the bad boys? The question is pressing on me hard. I raise my hand.

"Everyone?" I ask.

Sister Louise stares at me. "Yes, Jocelyn. You will have to confess too."

I wonder what Sister Louise knows about me. Her voice goes on about Jesus making fish and Wonder bread, but I can't hear her words. The boys aren't listening either. Gabe is playing baseball with a piece of paper. Another boy is pretending to die.

Sister Louise moves around the wooden desks, layers of gray dress trailing. When she comes close to me, I tell her I have a stomachache. She waves her hand toward the door. She tells me to go wait for my mother on the swings. Church is ending. My mother sees me come out of the basement before catechism is over. She gives me the look that says, *This better be good, young lady.*

I try to explain about my stomachache. I ask, "What happens to you if you have a stained soul? If I die now, will I float in purgatory or . . ." I can't bring myself to finish my question.

Disgusted, my mother yanks me to the car by the arm. I should have listened better.

Mom sleeps late the following Sunday and the Sunday after that. Diane, the bossy girl, recognizes me on the playground at school. While I hang upside down on the monkey bars, she tells me that Sister Louise has said that I will not be able to make my First Communion if I do not come to Sunday school next week. I pull my shirt down to cover my belly button. And my stained soul.

That Sunday, I beg my mother to take me to Sunday school so that I can learn how to confess my sins and make my First Communion. I tell her that I will go to church with the O'Neils if she wants to sleep longer. She gets angry and tells me that it's not necessary to attend church. She tells me that God is love and that he is everywhere and that I can talk to him whenever and wherever I want to. "You don't need a priest, Jocelyn," she tells me.

I still don't understand.

"I've had it, Jocelyn. What crap." She gets up to make herself a cup of coffee.

I want to tell her all the terrible things I've done to stain my soul, but she's busy looking in the newspaper, trying to find out what kind of day Virgo will have, and I can't make myself begin.

THIRTEEN

I wake to my mother sitting on the edge of my bed, coffee cup and cigarette in hand. I'm still in the clothes I wore to the party. "Get changed, Jocelyn. We're going to church."

I haven't heard that in about ten years. I raise my eyebrows. Do we trust the God of church again? Will God make Gabe reappear?

"We're going to support the O'Neils. They need us."

I'm ashamed because instead of thinking about Gabe, I'm wondering what people wear to church now. Do they still dress up like they did when I was seven? Or are dresses out, like Latin Mass and hats? I decide to wear my embroidered shirt over my brown corduroys. No one will be able to tell that I'm in pants when I'm sitting in the pew.

We walk toward the church with the O'Neils. People have clustered on the front lawn and on the steps. A group of seniors stares at me for a minute. I'm not sure if it's because I'm with the entire O'Neil clan—Gabe's sister and brothers drove up from their homes to be with their parents this morning—or if it's because I'm not a practicing Catholic. Either way, they look away quickly, as if in looking at me they've broken a rule and they don't want to be caught. It isn't only the Amish who shun those who have strayed. I am invisible.

Once inside, my mother starts to put her hand in the holy water and then stops herself. The sign of the cross that she doesn't make hangs in the air like a song whose last note hasn't been sung. I want to complete it for her. I do an imaginary sign of the cross in my head. If I were to really cross myself, I'd probably do it backward.

We slide into a pew and wait. I look around surreptitiously. I wonder if Theresa has arrived. More truthfully, I need to know if Benny has. Where does he sit? Does he see me? What will his eyes say today? Will they send a message of longing? Will they joke a flat hello? So far, nothing.

There is the faint smell of incense. I breathe slowly, trying to pull that sweet smell deep inside me. I am taken back to little-girl times, sitting in the last pew. My mother has slipped in to avoid the stares of parishioners who seemed to say, *Either you're not divorced or you're not Catholic, which is it?* I remember sitting with a book, *The Little Golden Book of God,* on my lap, my feet swinging in red Mary Janes, slowly letting my eyes travel up one side of the church—all the way to Jesus nailed on the cross—and then back down the other side.

By the time my eyes reached the side opposite, the sun would have come up behind the mountains, pouring light through the stained-glass windows. The geometric faces of the Bible people would glow brighter. I'd stare at the windows until I no longer saw pictures, only strands of color, golden reds and yellows that fell across the cheeks and laps of parishioners. Even mine.

I stare at the stained glass now, trying to recapture that feeling of being touched by divinity. The faces look vaguely familiar, but I can't remember the names or the stories, except for the birth and crucifixion of Christ. I look at the compassionate eyes of Mary holding her baby boy. My gut tightens. I remember the words to a Christmas carol my grandmother used to sing: *Lullay my liking, my dear Son, my Sweeting.* For the first time I am hit by what Margo must be feeling. I look up at the high beams and say a prayer in my head. It isn't the first prayer I've uttered since leaving the Church, but it's still awkward. In here God and I are strangers.

Theresa slides into the pew next to me and puts her head on my shoulder for a moment. She's a funny Catholic. She doesn't get hung up on the pope's laws the way Benny does. She says that she likes going to church. She likes knowing that she's part of a tradition that's thousands of years old. But when she lost her virginity to Sam, a guy who attends community college, she didn't confess. "It's none of Father Warren's business," she said assuredly. "What would he know about such things, anyway?"

I get through the service remembering—and not remembering. Standing, kneeling, sitting one beat after everyone else. Wishing for a moment that I belonged and at the same time scornful of the beliefs that forced us out. Remaining with my mother while worshippers around us rose for Communion.

The service ends, and I wish that Theresa and I could find something to do together, but she's singing with her family, an occasional performing troupe, at the state hospital in Concord. She says good-bye to me on the front steps, and I cup my hands above my eyes to spot my mother and the O'Neils in the slowly emerging crowd.

That's when I hear my name.

"Jossee."

Just the way I like it. I turn to look at Benny.

"How are you?" he asks.

"I'm okay," I say. I walk slowly over to the side of the crowd near the little cemetery, hoping Benny will follow. He does, but his hands are in his pockets and his eyes stay on the flock.

"How are *you* doing?" This is the question. I feel like my life is hanging here.

"Okay," he says. Which tells me nothing.

"How's your mother?" I ask.

"Better this morning, but she didn't feel well enough for church. Father Warren will come out and give her the sacraments later."

"Lucky you," I say. "Church twice." I sound more cynical than I mean to.

"Any ideas about Gabe?" he asks.

"Not a one. I feel like I should be doing something, but I don't know what."

Benny still watches the door. I wonder who he's looking for.

Father Warren comes out of the church and begins to shake the hands of parishioners.

"I better run," says Benny. "I'm chopping wood this afternoon."

Sounds like a quick dismissal. Only I know it's an invitation.

FOURTEEN

We're seven years old. My mother tells me to put on any old dress and get in the car. We are going to watch Gabe, who still gets to be Catholic, make his First Communion. Just as we arrive it is Gabe's turn to go into the confessional booth. I hold my breath as he disappears behind the black curtain. *What will he say first? What will the priest say? What will Gabe's punishment be?* His father is standing with Gabe's sister and brothers, who are jumping in the aisle of the church. He gives Gabe's brother Timmy a look that says, *Cut it out.* Timmy stops cold. I can't hear Margo and my mother's talk; I hear only a ringing in my ears.

Finally, Gabe and the priest come out together. Father pats Margo on the shoulder. Then he shakes Mike's hand and says, "You have another fine boy here, Mike." Gabe is grinning from ear to ear. His mother hugs him. His father smiles. Gabe has a shiny white soul.

I watch the other girls wear angel dresses, carry white flowers with ribbons, and walk with Gabe. I hear Father talk about how God loves these children and how he will guide them in all that they do. When Father gives Gabe a taste of wine, I picture the windows beside me opening wide. Giant moths soar in to capture me with my grubby stained soul and fly me right out of there.

FIFTEEN

At home I change into my painter pants and head for the kitchen. I decide to make the O'Neils my famous brownies. It's not that I think brownies are the best thing to eat when you're suffering, it's just that they're the only thing I know how to bake. I dump out a package of brownie mix, mix in oil and two eggs. Then I add my secret ingredient, a cup of chocolate chips.

My mother, the O'Neils, and Father Warren are seated in the living room of the O'Neil house when I walk in. Most of the adults are staring off, seemingly lost in their own thoughts. Gabe's sister, Mary, is crying. She stands when she sees me.

"Little Jocelyn. I remember babysitting you when you were this big." She lowers her hand near the floor.

Thanks a lot. I put my brownies on the coffee table. Father Warren smiles at me. So does Mom. She's pleased that I'm doing something.

"I can't take another minute of this!" shouts Gabe's father. He walks out of the room and grabs his baseball cap and a jacket off a hook in the hallway.

"Where are you going?" Margo calls.

"I gotta go looking. Anywhere. For all we know, Gabe could be lying in the woods somewhere bleeding to death."

"Mike," says Father Warren calmly, but he doesn't move from his chair.

Margo jumps up to prevent Father Warren from saying one word about having faith. "I'll come with you," she says. But Mike shakes his head no, and Margo stays.

I wait in the O'Neils' kitchen for a while. But there is nothing to do. The police haven't called. There is no news at all. I feel like a Peeping Tomasina or something.

I walk out the door, take my old English bike out of the shed, and head for the woods.

An orange strip of plastic hanging on a tree marks the patch of woods I'm looking for. I slow down, hop off my bike, and walk it down the narrow path. The grass and plants that mark the recently cut lane are bright green. I spot new shoots that will blossom into lady's slippers—flowers that are near extinction and are forbidden to pick.

Benny is exactly where I knew he would be. He

has a small chain saw, and he's concentrating on taking the limbs off a large fallen tree. His father bought
a few acres of land off the highway coming into town.
Benny spends his free time collecting firewood for the
winter. He's already piled cords and cords. It helps
him work off frustration about his mom, I think.

I park my bike next to his father's truck and walk
slowly into his line of vision. I don't want to startle
him.

He sees me and stops the saw. I can tell by his eyes
that he's glad I've come.

"Hiya," he says.

"Hi." I can barely talk above a whisper.

"You're a surprise." We both know he's lying.
We've been through this before. I know that he hoped
I'd come. In order for Benny and me to be together, I
have to take the initiative. It has to be out of his
hands. He has to lose control.

He puts the chain saw down and turns toward me.
"Any news?" he asks.

"None," I say. There's silence. I can tell that Benny's
thinking about what to say next.

"How are you doing?" he asks.

I smile a sad smile.

"I've always thought that you had a thing for Gabe."
His eyes are slightly mischievous, challenging me.

"What makes you think that?" I don't talk about

Gabe when I'm with Benny—unless I happen to be telling a story from a hundred years ago.

"I guess Anna Beal had a thing for him too," he says.

It's strange that he mentions Anna and not Bernadette. I sense a bit of longing in this statement, and I want to say, *So what's it to you?* I look up at the sky. I wish I hadn't come.

"I gotta go," I say.

"You just got here."

"From the looks of it," I say, glancing over at his measly pile of cuttings, "so did you."

"Yeah, you think you could cut faster?"

"Of course," I say. "You forget that I was conceived in these New Hampshire woods."

Benny blushes. I love it when he does that.

"Ever used a chain saw?"

"No. But it can't be that hard."

"Come here," he says. I walk over to where he's standing. He wraps his arms around me from behind to show me how to use the saw. His hands are guiding my hands. I can't concentrate. All I can do is smell the sweet soap smell of Benny mixed with pinewoods and feel the warmth of the sun on the back of my neck. My insides are swelling.

I turn to look up at him. *Please kiss me, Benny,* I think. And he does. He pulls a straggly strand of hair off my face and kisses me—gently at first and then as long and as hard as we've ever kissed before. I bend away to drop the saw and then crawl under his shirt. He crawls under mine. His hands are cold, but only for a moment. We sink to the forest floor and roll in the taste of each other. We are on the log and under the log. Last fall's pine needles are in my hair and in my sneakers and in every gap of my painter pants. Benny and I push against each other so hard—we try to make our bodies one body. We succeed, I think.

Then we are still. Neither one of us wants to break the spell. I listen to a chickadee in the woods. For a moment I worry about the bargain Benny made with God. I hope he's decided that his mother's disease and being with me are unrelated.

I roll on top of Benny. I trace my fingers from his forehead down the bridge of his nose, over his soft lips, and down his neck. I outline the bottom of his neck, where wispy hairs grow. And that's when I realize something.

Benny sees my eyes and immediately puts his hand to his neck. He feels for his Saint Christopher's medal, but the chain isn't there. He bolts up.

"Did you put it on this morning?" I ask.

"Oh, Christ," he says. "I never take it off!"

We spend close to an hour searching the ground in and around the fallen tree. The medal is gone.

There is nothing I can say. Benny's distracted. He halfheartedly promises that he'll stop by the Grill tomorrow. But I know as I throw my leg over my bicycle and head toward home that we're dealing with a major sign.

SIXTEEN

The end of the school day. The teacher tells the walkers to line up. It is Tuesday, the day that Gabe and I go to Mrs. Cavanaugh's after school, so I grab my lunch box and my corrected papers and stand up. Bobby asks if I will be his walker buddy. I nod my head and stand next to him. Gabe, who is first in line, is looking for me. "Who is your walker buddy, Gabe?" asks the teacher.

"Jocelyn," says Gabe. "Jocelyn is *always* my walker buddy."

The teacher looks at me. I look at Bobby.

Bobby says, "You can be Gabe's buddy, Jocelyn."

At that moment I know my mother is wrong. You don't catch more flies with honey. Bobby is one of the sweetest boys in my class, but I happily take my place with Vinegar.

The walker-patrol kid with an orange sash on his

chest directs us across a busy intersection on Main Street. Then the buddy line breaks up, and kids go their separate ways. Gabe walks slightly ahead of me. We walk down the hill past Ray's Market, past the Grill, over the bridge, and up the hill to Mrs. Cavanaugh's.

We run the last five hundred yards, trying to beat each other through the door. Gabe's hand slaps the screen first. He goes directly to the pink snowball cupcakes on the table. I tell Mrs. Cavanaugh about the New Hampshire report I completed in school. I tell her that the report got a blue star on it. My first one. But when I rifle through the papers I've clutched all the way home, the booklet is missing.

"Go back and trace your steps," Mrs. Cavanaugh says. "Your mother will want to see your fine work."

I turn around and look at Gabe.

"You too, Gabe. Go back and help Jocelyn find her report."

Gabe stands there and stares at Mrs. Cavanaugh. His chocolaty mouth is wide open. *You've got to be kidding,* his eyes challenge.

"Go on."

He grabs his jacket in a huff, and we head back down the hill. "You are such a pansy," he says. I ignore him.

We can see that there is nothing on the sidewalk

between Mrs. Cavanaugh's and the bridge. I want my report back desperately, but I'm afraid to make Gabe climb the rest of the way back to school.

"It must have blown over the bank," says Gabe. "Where else could it be?" He slides down the steep, muddy bank on his rear end. "Come on, Jocelyn. It's your stupid report."

I follow. I tell myself that he could be right. The report could have blown down here. We have a reason for being in this forbidden place.

We walk along the edge of the water. The river is more powerful here than downstream, where we live. Here in town, we're at the foot of the falls. Water pounds; foam from the mill swirls and splatters.

I search under every bush. I pick up a stick and throw it into the churning river. Gabe does the same. Our sticks battle the surface for a moment and then dive only to come up somewhere closer to our homes.

I look up. "Where are you going?" I yell to Gabe, who is scrambling over brush.

"To the bridge. Come on!"

I'm afraid. We're supposed to be searching for my report. I want to find it. I don't want to go where we're not supposed to go, but I follow. I've already been called a pansy once today; I'm not going to give Gabe another reason to tease me.

Gabe crawls up onto the rusted platform, high

above the falls below. He stands and holds out his hand. I hesitate.

"Come on, Jocelyn."

I take his hand and tentatively step from bar to bar, afraid that I'll fall between the gaps. He leads me to the edge, which is supported by the iron railing, and we lean into the spray. I feel the mist on my face and giggle. Gabe raises himself up onto the bars and leans over. I know I can't stop him, so I hold on to his belt just in case.

The sun is beginning to set. When I look at Gabe, he is a black silhouette. Yet, he glows.

Gabe feels me watching him. He feels me holding on to him. He extends his arms wide and leans farther over the falls.

"I'm flying. Look, Jocelyn, I'm flying."

SEVENTEEN

I'm eating beef stew at the table with Mom. She pulls a crumpled leaf from my hair.

"I haven't seen Benny around for a while," she says.

"He's been busy—with his mom and all. Plus, he's looking for a summer job."

"Did you see him today? Jocelyn?" She's picking at the potatoes in the bottom of the bowl. I know she's trying to make her dinner last as long as this conversation needs to.

I take a heaping spoonful and nod.

"Where did you see him?"

"Church."

"And?"

"On his land. He was chopping wood."

"I hope you're being careful, Jocelyn," she says. "I hope you're remembering what I told you."

I can't have this conversation now. I'm already so confused. I don't know if Benny has changed his mind about what's right and what's wrong. I don't know if I'm going with Benny now or not. I have no idea what he feels about today. I have no idea what *I* feel about today.

I realize that for a few short months I felt like a normal high school kid. I had a best friend. I had a boyfriend. When Margo crowed about Gabe's plans for a Friday night, my mother had something to say about me. And now Benny is changing his mind.

"You don't want to end up with a reputation like Bernadette's," Mom says. "If you keep running after Benny, Jocelyn, that's the reputation you're going to get."

I feel punched. The same mother who told me to take charge, to get a prescription for the Pill if I felt I was ready, is telling me this? Is this what she thinks? That I'm a slut?

Mom fumbles in her purse, takes out a cigarette, and lights up. She hasn't smoked for a long time, and now twice in one day. I know she's scared, scared about Gabe, scared about me, but I can't help her.

I pick up my bowl, leave it on the counter, and head toward the hall.

"I just don't want you to end up like me, Jocelyn," Mom snips as I climb the stairs.

Don't worry, I think. *It isn't likely that a baby will ruin my life, the way I've ruined yours.*

EIGHTEEN

Mrs. Morrin, our fourth-grade teacher, tells us that a new girl—a girl all the way from Maryland—will be joining us. Like most of the kids in my class, I'm excited. A new girl means that the day will be livelier, that our teacher will be kinder. She will pretend to take time to consider which child should be the new girl's helper. *After all,* she will seem to say, *we are a model class and the decision is difficult.* But in the end, she will choose Susan, who is nearly perfect.

She will not choose me because I am untidy—my mother doesn't always have time to help me with my straggly hair or make sure I don't wear the same dress two or three days in a row. Mrs. Morrin also thinks I ask too many questions. "*Think* for once, Jocelyn," she says. And I know that someone will be quick to tell the new girl that my parents are divorced. I am the only fourth grader whose father doesn't live with her, and this fact will be presented along with the knowledge that there's a crazy woman who wails behind Ray's Market. Both of us should be avoided.

But I am still hopeful. Maybe this new girl, maybe this Anna Beal will be a friend. So I raise my hand when Mrs. Morrin says, "Who would like to be Anna's helper?" and I continue to smile at the new girl long after Susan has been chosen.

I like Anna. She is smarter than I am, and braver, too. She seems to like all of the fourth-grade girls the same, even though Susan tells her which girls are the popular ones. I invite Anna over to my house after school to hunt for salamanders and frog's eggs in the brook that feeds the river farther down the road. She asks if we can look for snakes in the stone wall. I'm afraid of snakes, but I don't tell Anna that—Anna who can do push-ups and whose knees are rough and grimy like a boy's.

I like Anna, that is, until I discover how much Gabe likes Anna. When Anna comes to my house, Gabe sits in front of us on the bus and makes silly jokes. He hurries inside his house to get his snack, and then he runs over to my backyard to eat it. He tries to interest us in games of kick the can and capture the flag. Anna smiles and points out that we really don't have enough kids to play those games. Gabe seems pleased that she knows the names of these games and how to play them. As if Anna from Baltimore wouldn't know the same games as Gabe in Weaver Falls.

When Anna isn't with me, Gabe comes over and asks questions about her. Then he tells me all the things they have in common. Both of them like blue best. Both of them hate beets. Both of their mothers make them wash their necks before going to bed. Both of them are Catholic.

I'm confused. I want to be with Gabe, but hearing about Anna makes it hard to breathe. Gabe gives Anna a birthday present—a picture puzzle of daisies. Anna writes Gabe a thank-you note. Gabe circles the word *love* in *I love my puzzle* and in *Love, Anna,* and he hangs the note on his wall. He brings me up to his room, a place that I haven't been invited to since I was six, to see the letter hanging there. "Tell Anna," he says.

NINETEEN

The parking lot of the Grill is filled with cars, and the sun is barely up. I count three police cruisers and five cops holding dogs by leashes.

"'Bout time you got here," Joe says. He's pouring coffee. Linda is flipping eggs.

"What's going on?" I ask as I tie my apron around my waist. I am not late.

"The town decided to organize a search for Gabe this morning."

"Have they discovered something? Where are they going to look?" Woods and mountains surround the town. I wonder if they plan to cover it all.

"They're going to start in the woods behind St. Mary's," says Joe. "Here, take these eggs to Father Warren."

I look behind me and see him at a corner table. He's sitting with three kids—a senior who just graduated and two kids from my class.

He smiles at me when I place his breakfast in front of him.

My belly does a little flip. For a moment I forget what I need to do next, then I back over to the dirty table Joe's busing. The guys at the table laugh as soon as I'm gone.

"Is Father Warren here to say a prayer for the search?" I ask.

"I don't think so," Joe says. "Someone saw Gabe coming out of the back of St. Mary's around midnight the night he went missing."

I clear some coffee mugs and wonder what Gabe would be doing in the back of the church.

"Was he alone?" I ask, following Joe to the sink.

"Well, no one has confessed to being with him, and no one else has turned up missing."

"They think he was there to steal something," Linda mumbles over her shoulder.

I serve two men seated at the counter. One was my eighth-grade English teacher. I try to think of what Gabe could steal.

"The collection money?" I ask Linda when she hands me some toast.

"Nope. The only thing missing was a couple of bottles of Communion wine."

As if on cue, all of the men and some of the women in the Grill throw down their napkins. They stand up and put on their hooded sweatshirts. Some carry topographical maps. They hook canteens over their shoulders or adjust canteens on their belts. The dogs outside begin to wag their tails and pull on their leashes. They can hear that it's time to go.

I help Linda load the dishwasher. "That poor family," she says.

I try to piece the information together, but it's a puzzle that won't fit. "So they think Gabe got so drunk . . ."

"That he's laying comatose—or, worse, dead—in the woods behind the church," she says.

"Isn't this a pretty big search party to discover Gabe dead behind the church?"

Linda hands me a spatula with which to clean the griddle. "He may not have passed out immediately. He may have gotten lost back there. He may have gone down toward the river or up into the mountains. If we're lucky, he's simply lost in the hills."

I imagine Gabe up in the mountains. They aren't big, but you could go in circles for days, and in some places it's twenty miles to the nearest town. It's June; he could survive if he's lost.

"Was Father Warren the one who saw Gabe coming out of the church?" If so, I can't believe that he would wait this long before telling someone.

"No," Linda says. "The police got a call from one of Father's neighbors."

The Grill is busy all day. People want to be nearby. Lots of people want to help, but they don't know what to do. Women deliver meals for the O'Neils, and children draw them pictures. Older men come to talk about the time they got lost hunting in those hills and how frightening an experience it was. Theresa comes and asks Joe if she can waitress too. He looks at her as if she's daft. Joe has never liked Theresa. He calls her a braless women's-libber. Her parents, bleeding-heart liberals. But today is a different day. He tosses her an apron.

From time to time, I check the clock. No Benny.

Around six, men and women who have been out searching come straggling back. Family members meet them with warmer jackets. Joe, Linda, Theresa, and I serve steaming cups of coffee. No one wants to call it a day.

A few wives have brought candles and pictures of Gabe cut from the newspaper or in photographs with their own children. They start to build a little shrine for him on the counter. They place small signs among the pictures that say things like, HANG ON, SWEETIE.

"Hey, everybody, pipe down!" Joe says as the story comes over the little TV set hung in one corner.

A reporter is shown interviewing members of the search party as they emerge from the woods. They say gallant things, but their faces betray their words. They interview Mike, and he faces the camera to talk to Gabe directly. He urges him to call home if he can, and if he can't, not to lose hope. "I promise you, we'll find you, son."

That night I drift in and out of a restless sleep. At one point I am jolted from a nightmarish dream by the sound of something hitting my window. Rain? If so, it stops abruptly. I get up and look out. The night is starry, not a cloud. Looking down, I see a tall figure with a lit cigarette next to the willow tree. Who is it? Does he see me? Oh, my God. Gabe!

I sneak down the stairs and out the back door. I stand in the side yard, in the dark, and call his name. No one is there.

TWENTY

Kids in my fifth-grade class have stopped taking the bus home in the afternoon. Instead, they walk home so they can stop off at St. Mary's cemetery. Each morning as I hang up my jacket and put my lunch in the coat closet, I hear whispers and giggles about the day before. I long to be a part of this expedition.

One day I tell my mother that I will be walking home that afternoon. She looks at me suspiciously but says that she supposes it will be okay, as long as I'm careful. I leave the classroom and walk out with the walkers. Buddies are no longer required; now we are just one swarming, buzzing crowd.

"Would you like to walk home together?" I ask Anna.

She blushes and says awkwardly, "I can't, Jocelyn. Sorry. I've promised others," and runs to catch up.

I walk slowly past the cemetery, but the kids are already out of sight. Are they behind the church? Did they go into the church? I think about trying to find them, but I don't dare.

That Saturday, I wander over to Gabe's. The bulkhead doors are open. Gabe is playing records in the basement. I cautiously invite myself down. He keeps playing a song called the "Ballad of the Green Berets." It's a sad song, a song about men jumping from airplanes and dying, the kind of song that carves a deep pit in your stomach, and we listen to the record over and over until we've memorized the words.

When the needle slides to the scratchy center of the record once again, I ask the question that I've been rehearsing in my mind. "What do you do at the cemetery?"

Gabe looks embarrassed. "Fool around," he says.

"Fool around doing what?" I ask.

"Watch." Gabe turns so his back is facing me. He crosses his arms and hugs himself, but from behind it looks as if someone is hugging him. Then he moves his head in a romantic way so it looks as if he's making out with someone. I crack up.

"What else do you do?" I ask.

"Come here, I'll show you."

I get off a stool and go and sit on a musty old couch. Gabe tells me to put my hand over my mouth.

Then he puts his hand over his mouth, and we pretend to kiss. Not a quick kiss like my mother used to give me when she said good night, but a long, rolling-around kiss like they do in the movies.

Gabe's laughing and I'm laughing and we're still pretend kissing.

"Now take your hand away," says Gabe.

I stare down at my hand as if it might show some evidence of our game.

That's when Gabe places his lips on mine. We roll around again, but this time our hands are gone. Our lips are really touching.

After a minute or so Gabe gets up and walks out into the sunlight. I follow him.

Matthew is in the backyard forcing a push mower around the yard.

"What were you two doing down there?" he asks.

"Practicing," says Gabe.

TWENTY·ONE

Theresa's about to take me home from the Grill when Benny pulls up in his father's sedan. "Can you go for a drive?" he asks.

"Theresa was coming over," I say, trying to be both strong for me and loyal to my best friend. "She was going to spend the night."

"That's all right, Jocelyn," she says. "I probably should see if they need me at the co-op."

I thank Theresa with my eyes and get in the car. Benny is in jeans and an old T-shirt and still carrying the grime of the day.

"Where do you want to go?" I ask.

"Let's get an ice cream at Willie's."

I've been making milk shakes at the Grill all day, and ice cream interests me as much as a spoonful of grease right now. But I'm relieved to be with Benny.

We walk into the bright and busy ice-cream

parlor and are directed to a corner table. "I should call Mom," I say. I head for the pay phone. I don't have a dime, so I call collect.

Mom takes the call and says that she hopes I'll come home soon. Everybody wants his or her family close. I watched mothers kiss the tops of kids' heads all day today.

Benny tells me that he helped with the search. He hiked with some of the ballplayers at the base of Mason's Mountain. "It's hard," he says. "You keep your eyes down, hoping that you'll find something. At the same time you hope you won't find anything—anything that might show that he's hurt or maybe even dead. I mean, everyone's talking about Gabe being lost. But nobody's mentioning that he might have been murdered."

"God, Benny. Why would anyone want to murder Gabe? You've spent too much time in the big city."

"What do you mean?" he says, mocking himself. "You're a big fan of daytime TV. You know anything can happen in a small town like Weaver Falls."

Benny orders vanilla ice cream. I order root beer. "Did you find your Saint Christopher?" I ask, trying to bring the subject closer to us.

He shakes his head no. "But I saw Father Warren today. I asked him where I could find another one. Like the one my mother had bought me."

"What did he say?"

"He said that he would take me to a jewelry store in Keene."

"Why is he going to take you?" I ask. Benny can borrow the car. He could take me.

I hate to admit it. I get jealous of Father Warren sometimes. Actually, I don't get jealous of him. I get jealous of the guys who hang out with him. It seems like one more club that I can't belong to. I wish I had a priestly friend who would take me to buy a medal for spiritual protection.

"You know how Father Warren is," Benny says.

"Did you tell him how you lost the medal?" I kid. I want Benny to remember yesterday.

He nods his head. "Yep," he says.

Is he joking? I wait to see that light in his eyes that tells me he's teasing. But it doesn't come. "You did?" I say. He couldn't have. *Please tell me, Benny, that you didn't tell Father Warren about yesterday.*

Benny can see that I've got a real problem with this, so he suggests that I finish my drink and we head back to the car. He asks for the bill, pays the waitress, leaves a tip. It all happens in slow motion.

I am so mad, so hurt, by the time I get to the car, I can't speak. I feel betrayed. I know if Benny can tell Father Warren about us, he can give us up. You don't share this kind of information with a priest so he'll praise you for good behavior. We sit there in the parking lot.

Benny sighs loudly. "Jocelyn, it's not like I have a choice."

"What do you mean you don't have a choice?"

"Father Warren comes to my house. He talks to my mother, he gives her the sacraments. Then he wants to talk to me."

"Why?"

"He wants to know how I'm doing. He asks if I'm helping out. It's hard to talk in front of my mother, so he asks me to walk him to the car. Sometimes we sit in the driveway, sometimes we drive around, but he always ends up asking me questions."

"What kind of questions?"

"Questions about everything. He wants to know how I'm getting on in Weaver Falls. He wants to know who my friends are."

"And you've told him about me?" I ask.

"Yes," says Benny. He says it like he's ashamed.

"And what does Father Warren say about me?"

"He reminds me of things."

"What things?"

"He thinks I should stay away from you, Jocelyn."

"He said that? He said that you should stay away from me?" Suddenly, I'm outside of my body.

It's like I'm up in the air somewhere looking down on Benny and me.

"Yes. He thinks I should get a job this summer. He thinks I should play baseball next year."

"Do you even like baseball?"

"Yes, as a matter of fact," he says. "Not that I'm great at it or anything."

For a moment I wonder if Benny didn't go out for the high school team last semester so he could spend more time with me. "But other guys do those things and still go out with girls. Right?"

Benny just nods. There is something he's not telling me.

"What exactly does Father Warren say about me, Benny?"

He doesn't answer me.

I tell him to take me home.

He does.

I get out of the car and shut the door, softly.

He drives off.

I walk around to the back of the house. Mom is sitting on the steps of the back deck watching the sunset. She has her arm around Margo, who looks like she's been given something to make her sleep. Only she can't.

I want to walk over there and share some new

and important information that I've picked up. I could tell her that I thought I saw Gabe outside my window, but what would that do except frustrate her? Or give her false hopes? And who's to say that I didn't imagine the whole thing?

I half wave to them and walk down to the river. The sun sets on the front side of our house, but it's reflected in the water. I sit on a large boulder, on the grassy edge of the water, and hold my knees close to me. I hear mosquitoes in my ear. They buzz, *Benny, Benny, Benny.*

Gabe has disappeared. For a moment I wish I could too.

TWENTY TWO

Our bus arrives at school only to be turned around again. A water pipe broke. We'll have to make the day up in June, but who cares? Right now it's the end of September, and we're having an Indian summer.

Gabe and I wander into the backyard. He wants to talk about Anna. He tells me how he admitted that he liked her and she admitted that she liked him, so now they're going together. But he doesn't know what he should do. He hasn't kissed her yet, and her parents won't let her go to the movies or anything. Anna isn't allowed to date until she's sixteen.

"What *do* you do?" I ask.

"I sit next to her in youth group," he tells me.

"Oh, whoop!" I tease, and he chases me. I head down the hill for speed, but the river blocks me. He lunges and takes hold of my wrist, but he doesn't know what to do with me.

"Let's go down to Kiddy Brook," he says.

We walk down the road a stretch and head into the woods. Gabe's brothers showed us long ago where the water flows off the hills on its way to the river. We follow a narrow ribbon of water until it leads to a larger ribbon broken up by little islands. We are Huck Finn and Tom Sawyer. I tell Gabe that I'm going to build a raft.

Gabe looks at me like I'm nuts. He's not buying my transformation, but he confronts me with practical details. "Even if you could find the logs, what are you going to tie them together with?" he asks.

"Vines."

"This isn't a jungle. Where are you going to find vines?"

"I'm sure there are some kind of vines. Maybe I'll use thin branches." I find a fallen ash tree, a log just the size for my raft, and I begin pulling on it. The tree doesn't budge. High winds may have pushed this tree over, but it's keeping its grasp on the earth.

Gabe laughs at me. "Come on, strong girl," he says.

"I am strong," I say without really thinking about whether I am or not. I'm enjoying the attention.

"Yeah?" Gabe walks over to me. "Let me feel your muscle."

"Let me feel yours first," I say.

Gabe unbuttons the cuff of his white oxford shirt

and folds his arm. I look at his tight fist and the way he can make his veins stick out. His muscle bulges.

"Feel it," he says. I don't know how to feel a muscle, so I poke it with a finger. I am amazed at how solid it is. He laughs.

"Now let's see your muscle!"

I try to tighten my arm the way Gabe did. Barely a bump emerges from my scrawny eleven-year-old arm. Gabe howls.

"Let me feel it," he says, placing his thumb beneath my arm and his fingers above. He squeezes and I lurch away. It tickles.

"Ooh, you are a strong girl."

"I am!" I head over to a birch log and position my weight to pick it up. I pull with all my might. The log has rotted through, and I go stumbling backward.

Gabe and I are both laughing now.

"And if you get this raft together, where are you going to float to? The brook is blocked by rocks just down a ways."

"It is?"

"Yeah, I'll show you." We follow the brook through a culvert under the road and around a bend. There we come to a place where rocks have either piled up or been placed to form a little pool about three feet deep.

"Wow," I say. The sun is high; the water looks so inviting. "I wish we could swim."

"Why can't we?"

I look down. I am still in my Girl Scout uniform, complete with green kneesocks, sash, beret, and badges. My mother complained about the price of the uniform and the necessary accessories. She would kill me if I swam in it.

"Let's go undie-dipping," says Gabe.

I look at him to see if he's kidding.

"Why not?"

I don't know what to say. I've just come to the conclusion recently that it's probably not okay to change in front of Gabe anymore.

"Our underwear is the same as our bathing suits."

True. "You first," I say.

"Okay." Gabe strips down to his Skivvies, as he calls them, and begins to walk into the water. I notice red marks on his back and think about how they got there.

"Augh!" Gabe lifts his ribs and groans. The sun may be hot, but the nights are cold, and the water is too.

I take my uniform off and toss it onto a bush. I keep on my undershirt and underpants. Gabe's right. It does look as if I've got a bathing suit on. I carefully wade into the water.

At first we stay to the shallow edges or walk on rocks. We turn stones over to see salamanders. Our feet become scarlet and numb, then our legs. Before you know it, we're sliding in and out of the water on our bellies, winding and rolling like otters. We take turns holding our breath underwater. We spurt water between the spaces in our teeth. We splash and grab each other's ankles.

Eventually, we crawl up onto a grassy island and flop onto our backs. The edge of Gabe's hand touches mine. We look up at the downy sky and dry in the sun. School was canceled, the day is warm, and Gabe and I have had a secret adventure. I don't remember being happier.

TWENTY THREE

Summer has been put on hold. For a week now, crowds of people concerned about Gabe meet at the Grill. I can't remember what day it is. Joe and Linda haven't even mentioned me taking a regular day off like I'm supposed to. Theresa stops by the Grill early. I think she plans on helping out again, but she's on her way to the Mason Playhouse. She got a part in a summer theater production, in *Godspell.* She's psyched, but she's trying not to look happy around the crowd of rescue workers.

Benny comes in too. He joins a table of jocks in their now usual corner. Normally, they would be working at summer jobs, but instead, they act as if they're assigned to a detective case. A case with very few clues. Benny gives me a half smile and holds my eyes long. It's his way of being intimate and non-committal at the same time.

Linda's back working the grill. Joe tries to help her and fill in for Gabe. I have to take the order at Benny's table.

"So what's the difference between a boiled egg and a poached egg? What's the difference between sunny-side up and sunny-side down?" the jocks ask.

I can't tell if they are laughing with me or at me. My armpits are sweating inside my uniform, and I wonder if Benny has confided in them. A week ago I would have said no way, he cares about me. But now that he's told Father Warren everything there is to know, I can't tell. Maybe they think I'm the next sure thing.

It takes a long time to get their order.

Joe sees this and comes over. He puts his arm around me and says, "This girl's too good for you. You know that, don't you?" He's looking right at Benny.

I'm dying. Wish Joe would walk away. Wish he wouldn't move his finger up and down my neck. Wish I could disappear.

"I know," says Benny. Then he looks away. He seems genuinely pained.

After lunch Linda says I need to go on break. "It's the law," she tells Joe. Then she tells me that I can take tomorrow off and every Wednesday hereafter.

I walk over to Ray's Market and use the pay

phone to call the playhouse. Someone gets Theresa for me.

"Can we go somewhere after work?" I ask. "Anywhere."

Theresa picks me up right on time. I have never been so happy to see her Beetle. She drives me home so I can change out of my uniform and lies on my bed, picking at the chenille on the spread while I change. I throw on some gym shorts and an old camp T-shirt.

"Don't wear that," she says. "Let's go somewhere nice."

"We don't have anywhere nice to go."

"Let's go over to the inn in Jefferson. I heard there's a great guitar player there."

I give Theresa my "spill it" look. Clearly, someone in the summer theater group tipped her off to this guitar player. And if my guess is right, it isn't the guitar player she's interested in, but the one with the tip.

"Come on, Jocelyn, give me a little credit. There's more to life than hanging around with a bunch of small-town bums and drinking sloe gin fizzes."

I know she longs to be more sophisticated. I know that her family is more artsy than most in this town. But for some reason, I can't let her off so easily.

"So what are we going to do? Go to this inn and drink sloe gin fizzes?"

"Not likely," she says, ignoring my attempt at irony. "They'll card us for sure. Let's just go because it's different."

I can give her that. I want different too. I change into a jean skirt and macramé vest, leave Mom a note, and we're out of there.

I'm glad that we've come. I feel older and wiser entering the pub. The waitress is really nice—acts like we're adults when she brings us our Cokes. She and Theresa talk about the guitar player, whose name is Daniel. He's pretty talented. He has a six-string and a twelve-string and goes back and forth between the two. Sometimes he plays classical music, sometimes folk songs. I like them both.

There aren't many people in the room, and at first it seems normal. We got there pretty early. But as the night goes on the room remains fairly empty. So after every song it's just the two of us clapping and Daniel smiling back at us. Both Theresa and I start to feel self-conscious and silly—like we're Daniel groupies or something.

When he takes a break, we nod to each other and head out the front door. The night air is a cool pond. Theresa and I gulp. The air is free. We're free. We giggle our way into the car.

"So who didn't show up?" I ask.

Theresa smiles at me. "This kid who works on the sets. But that's okay. I'll see him tomorrow. Where do you want to go now?" She looks up in the mirror and flicks up the hair around her widow's peak. I love the way her hair makes the top of a heart on her forehead, but it drives Theresa nuts.

"We could go by Cumberland Farms."

"Why not." Theresa says it in a slightly resigned voice. Kids from Jefferson hang out in front of the convenience store, and sometimes kids from Weaver Falls join them. Even Father Warren has been known to make a stop now and then. Theresa knows that I know there's a smidgen of a chance that Benny will be there.

But he's not. Hardly anyone is.

"I wonder where the party is tonight," Theresa says.

"Do you want anything?" I ask, getting out of the car to buy Canada Mints.

"Two hunks, some excitement for a change. Think they have that inside?"

"I doubt it. But look." Theresa and I stare at the door as a girl our age, with a bag full of groceries and a carton of cigarettes, walks out.

It's Bernadette.

I jump back in. "Quick! Follow her!" I yell.

"Follow her?" Theresa's confused, but she starts the car anyway. Bernadette gets into a beat-up old

Buick and pulls out. We tail her, but not too closely.

I expect the station wagon to turn down any one of the maple-lined streets in the center of Jefferson, but Bernadette drives right out of town. "Maybe she's taking the groceries to Gabe," I say. "Maybe the two of them are camping out in the woods."

"Do you think they would? Would they stay hidden with everyone looking for him like that?"

"Maybe Gabe had a fight with his parents about Bernadette, and he said, 'Screw you. I'll be with her if I want to' and took off." I don't tell Theresa that Gabe may have gotten a belt or a fist before leaving.

"That doesn't make sense, Jocelyn. Think about it. The O'Neils would hate for anyone to think that they are less than perfect. Why would they get everyone involved if they had even the tiniest inkling that Gabe is shacked up with Bernadette somewhere?"

"You're right about that," I admit.

We turn onto a steep winding road. I switch off the radio that's playing a Beach Boys song. "California Girls" seems too obnoxious for this slow ascent. But without the music, the night is entirely too black, the road too deserted.

"Hey," I say. "Remember that story about the couple that goes parking? They make out, then the car won't start, so the guy says he'll go and get help. Remember?"

Theresa looks at me as if I have two heads.

"She locks all the doors and waits inside the car for an eternity. Then she hears this awful scratching on the roof. She screams, but no one hears her. In the morning help comes. She gets out of the car and discovers her boyfriend, stabbed, stretched out across the top."

Theresa flips the radio back on. "Jocelyn, I can't believe it. I can't believe that we're on this godforsaken road chasing a girl we don't even know and you're telling horror stories."

For some reason, I feel wired. Like I've had fifty cups of coffee. I don't know why. But another story pops into my head to replace the first one. It's a story I saw on a soap opera. Evil Girl is in love with Good Guy, but Good Guy has come to his senses and fallen in love with someone else. Only Evil Girl can't let him go—she's obsessed with having him. So she drugs Good Guy and keeps him hostage in a jail cell, where she cares for him.

I start to ask Theresa if she watched this soap when she was younger, and if so, how does she think this woman built a jail cell? And does she think Bernadette could be keeping Gabe hostage? But she stops the car suddenly, before I can ask.

I stare ahead.

"She turned in there," she says, pointing to a dirt driveway.

"Come on, then," I say, one hand on the door handle. "Let's go check it out."

"You've got to be kidding," says Theresa. "This is as far as I go."

"Some best friend," I say.

I can't believe my own bravery. I pull my poncho on over my clothes. I don't mind going alone. When it comes to Gabe, I've always made my own way.

TWENTY-FOUR

Gabe's family is having a big cookout in the backyard. We are celebrating Matt's graduation from high school. The yard is filled with relatives—particularly cousins—and a bunch of seniors who don't have family parties of their own to attend.

Gabe is spinning a basketball on the tip of his finger. He is showing off for his cousin Jay, who is also twelve. Jay is taller than both of us, has curly brown hair, a flat nose, and eyes that take absolutely no notice of me.

When the basketball spinning wears thin, Gabe challenges Jay to climb a tall tree near the river. You can tell that Jay, a Manchester boy, hasn't had much practice in tree climbing. He's more tough city kid than country jock. But he likes Gabe, admires him even, and hoists himself up—climbs pretty high. Gabe climbs to a branch just higher than the one Jay is perched on and yells down to me.

"Go get me a rope, Jocelyn."

I know we don't have a rope in our shed, so I wander into Gabe's. The door lets in just enough light to make out the lawn mowers and rakes, fishing poles and tarps. On the wall is a coil of thick rope. I lift it off the spike, wrap it around my shoulder, and carry it back to the tree.

"What the hell are you guys doing?" Mike yells.

Gabe doesn't bother to answer. He practically slides down the branches, grabs the rope, and shimmies back up.

I hope that he'll challenge me to climb with the rope, to join the two of them in the tree. But he doesn't. This is a boy game. I'm the fetch girl.

He ties one end of the rope around a large branch. Then he peels off his clothes to his shorts, carries the rope down and out to the branch that extends farthest across the river, gives a Tarzan call, and swings out over the water: a wide arc at first, then smaller. When the rope slows down, Gabe lets go. We watch the water splash up in the sunlight. Then he appears.

I take my first breath since he took hold of the rope. But I am still frightened for him. We've been told to never swim in the river. It is filled with foamy chemicals from the mill in Jefferson. I imagine these chemicals creating gruesome, snakelike creatures that lurk beneath the rippled surface.

"Get up here!" Mike shouts when Gabe walks up the riverbank.

Gabe can't stop grinning.

"This is your brother's party. Not yours. Do you *always* have to be the center of attention?" The crowd is silenced by Mike's outburst.

I am standing close enough to the grill to see the hurt, and then the anger, in Gabe's eyes.

"Come on, Gabe," says Jay. He couldn't care less about his uncle Mike.

Gabe follows Jay to the dock. They stand on the boat dock, whipping each other with wet towels and laughing. Each slap strikes harder than the one before. Jay doesn't seem to mind. He can dish it out too.

Mom hands me a bowl of macaroni salad to take into the house. "Make yourself useful, Jocelyn. It's getting dark."

TWENTY FIVE

I don't know what I expected. A big house, tennis courts, Doberman pinschers racing out to meet me. But what I see when I reach the last twist in the driveway, which is really no bigger than a path, I'm totally unprepared for.

Bernadette's station wagon is parked next to other cars—beaten cars that haven't run for a long time. In addition to cars, there's a ton of other stuff: a bent baby-carriage frame, a rusty tricycle. In the corner of the clearing—you can't really call it a yard— is a faded, torn, inflatable wading pool. Next to the pool is a dirty doll, its head cracked open.

The house isn't a house—it's a basement. Apparently, someone was going to build a house but ran out of money. Or decided that they would rather not pay property taxes. In New Hampshire you have to pay taxes only on a house, not on a foundation.

So instead of building, they tar-papered a roof over the foundation—a flat roof that should have been a floor. The tar paper is peeling off.

I am so astounded by what I see that it takes me a moment to realize I *can* see it. Bernadette flicks her headlights off and steps out of the car. She turns and looks right at me.

"Who are you? Why are you following me?" *This* is bravery, for other than moonlight, it's dark.

I realize that she can't identify me while I'm on the driveway. For a moment I think of running, just getting out of there. But I don't.

"It's Jocelyn," I say. "From Joe's Grill."

Her voice calms, but it doesn't soften. "What do you want?"

"I don't know. I wanted to see where you were going. I wondered if Gabe would be there."

Just then a deep voice bellows from the basement. "Bernadette, where are you? Who are you talking to?"

A man staggers up from the bulkhead. He walks upright but tilted backward. Like a bear not used to walking on its hind legs. He's enormous. "Is your mother home?" He slurs his words.

"Not yet, Daddy. She's still at work. I'm talking to a girlfriend. Just a girlfriend."

"Lemmee see your girlfriend." He says it like she brought home some juicy treat.

"I got your Winstons." She walks over and hands her father the carton the way a mother would hand a baby a set of keys to keep it from pitching a tantrum. I try to imagine Bernadette living in this cellar with that man. I try to imagine the mother who will be returning home. I try to imagine Gabe visiting her here.

The man takes the carton, bends over—seemingly to stop the world from spinning—and then heads back down.

"Obviously, Gabe's not here," Bernadette says to me.

Why "obviously"? I ask myself.

I feel lost. I realize that all this time Gabe has been living a life completely apart from me. Our childhood games, our family get-togethers, our working together at the Grill have nothing, not a thing to do with who Gabe is and the life he now leads. I have no idea why he dates Bernadette. It seems to me that if it was just about sleeping with her, he'd have had a one-night stand. That it would have ended long ago. Did he talk to her father when he picked her up for dates?

"Bernadette, there's a pack missing from this carton!" the man yells.

"They must have opened the carton at the store, Daddy. I'll go back and get another pack for you later." Bernadette takes the missing pack out of her peacoat pocket. "Want a cig?" she says.

I remember Theresa in the car. She's got to be worried by now. But, hell, she could have come with me, right? "Sure," I say.

Bernadette and I sit up on a boulder. She lights two cigarettes and hands one to me. I actually think the taste of cigarettes, especially the no-menthol ones, is disgusting. But I do what Theresa and I have been practicing. I take a drag and puff out some smoke rings. It's a cool little trick when you can't stand the feel of smoke in your lungs.

"I can't wait to get out of here," Bernadette says. "As soon as I finish school, I'm getting a job, renting a place, and moving my mother out."

"Does your mother want to leave?"

"She thinks she has nowhere else to go. But that's not true. She could go far, if she believed in herself."

I really admire Bernadette at this moment, and I want to tell her, but I'm too chicken. "You must be worried sick about Gabe," I say instead.

I feel her shrug. "I miss talking to him."

It doesn't feel like a complete answer. "Do you love him?" I ask, and immediately wish I could take it back. What a stupid thing to say. I've never even asked Theresa if she's loved someone—not in the way I mean now.

She takes a long drag on her cigarette. She's decided to ignore the question, I think. But she hasn't.

"No one gets me and Gabe. They think they do—they think they know all about us. But they don't know the first thing."

"Like what?"

I can see her debating with herself—it's written all over her face: *Should I tell her or not?* "Well, I'm a virgin, for one thing."

"You are?" I wish I could have prevented my amazement from showing.

I think that she's going to say more, but she doesn't. She has no need to explain things to me.

"My friend's back on the road," I say, stamping out my butt. "I better go." For some reason, I don't want Theresa to come down this driveway. How Bernadette is seen in Weaver Falls is her choice. I want to keep it that way.

"I'll walk you out," she says. It's clear that Bernadette would rather be anywhere than back in that cellar. As we approach the end of the driveway she backs away from me.

I reach out for the car door handle and ask, "Where do you think Gabe is?"

"At confession." She throws down the cigarette and taps it out with her Timberlands, expensive shit-kickers. She sees me staring at her boots.

"Gabe bought them."

"*Where* do you think he is?"

"Get in, Jocelyn." Theresa's had it.

I stand there. I want to know what Bernadette means.

"Ask Father Warren," she says. Then she turns to walk back.

"Hey!" I hear just as I'm getting into the car. I pop back out.

"I do," she calls.

It makes no sense to me.

"Love Gabe," she says. "But not the way you do."

TWENTY SIX

Gabe and I have been on summer vacation long enough to be bored, wishing that something would happen.

We're picking blackberries, stuffing them into our mouths and bickering over whose property they grow on. Gabe tells me his father planted these berries. I tell him he's wrong, that my grandfather said they were growing here back when he built this house for him and Grandma. My grandmother used to make blackberry jam.

Gabe pegs a blackberry at me.

I peg one back, but I'm a terrible aim. I try again. I miss.

"Want to go down to the brook?" I say. I am not sure what Gabe will say. It is one thing for us to be talking on the borders of our property. It is another to actually do something together in a public place. Gabe thinks for a minute. "Okay. But you have to keep this a secret."

At first I think that he wants to keep it a secret from Anna. They are going together, and she may not like the fact that he spends time with me. Then I think that he probably wants to keep this day a secret from everybody. Kids would never stop teasing him if they learned he'd spent the day with Cootie Girl. So I promise him that no one else will know.

"I won't tell."

But when we make our way down the road, over the brush, and into the woods that border the brook, I realize that Gabe may have been talking about a different secret altogether. Here, where the brook bends and the water collects in a little pool, is a rickety house. A stick-and-board house tall enough to stand in.

"Who built this?"

"Who do you think?"

"You did? When did you do this?"

"Well, actually, it began as Matt and Timmy's house. But I followed them one day, and they had to let me help. That makes it mine, too."

I can't believe how cool it is, but when I walk

inside expecting, I don't know, miniature furniture and a table set for tea, I'm disappointed. There are naked ladies on the walls, dirty magazines and beer cans on the floor, and the place smells like smoke and beer. The only things cool about the inside are some candles in tuna cans, a smiley-face water pillow, and a photograph of Gabe and his brothers taped above the door.

Gabe starts to show me some stuff in a wooden box. I lean over, and the cross I'm wearing dangles in front of my chin.

"You still have that?" he asks. He points to the gift his mother gave me the year I was supposed to make my First Communion. I sit up, and Gabe runs his finger along the chain.

"Here, give it to me," he says.

I look at him, confused.

"You're not even Catholic," he says. "You don't go to church. Why do you want a cross?"

I don't tell him that I still talk to God, that I hold the cross in my fingers when I pray. Gabe would tell me that I had forsaken God and that there's no way God would listen to the prayers of someone who had walked out on him. Suddenly, I feel like a fraud, like I'm pretending. Or, worse, like I'm wearing something that doesn't belong to me.

I take the cross off and hand it to Gabe. He refastens the chain and hangs it on a nail on the wall. The cross falls onto the breasts of a woman. Gabe laughs.

I smile. Not because of the woman, but because Gabe has shown me this house. Something of mine is on the wall. I belong.

TWENTY SEVEN

I'm not sure why I woke up with such clarity today. But seeing Bernadette has somehow made me see my own life more clearly. I can't believe that I've been feeling sorry for myself all these years with my father off doing whatever he pleases. I bet Bernadette would give anything for her father to get the hell out of there. Gabe must have seemed like a slice of heaven to Bernadette. Who wouldn't rather be in the arms of someone like Gabe than listening to a drunken father in a cellar hole? On the other hand, does she deserve Gabe's on-again, off-again attention?

Or do I deserve Benny's on-again, off-again attention?

I get myself a bowl of cereal and turn on *Days of Our Lives*. Julie was ready to divorce Bob for Doug, but now she's pregnant with Bob's child. So

Doug, wanting what's best for everyone, lies to her and tells her that he doesn't love her after all. Watching makes me feel more frustrated. Why does everything have to be so complicated?

I flick off the TV and run around the house like a madwoman, picking up the clutter, washing the scum off every surface. I keep singing the same song lyrics—*"Wake up with no will to carry on, morning you're not here, but never gone"*—over and over while I scrub.

"Change the station, Joss," my mother yells, like she always does when I have a tune stuck in my head.

I simply lower the volume.

"Oh, you're an angel," she says when she sees that I've cleaned up the house. "Shawnee is coming over to do a reading for Margo this afternoon."

"Won't Mike be furious?" I ask. Shawnee is a woman from my mother's psychic group. She's a medium, which means that when she reads tea leaves or tarot cards, she's getting messages from the Great Goddess or the Universal Mind (it doesn't really matter what you call it). Mike thinks that my mother's psychic group is dangerous, that it could make Margo forget God's intentions for women.

"I don't think Mike's in any position to judge

right now. I think he'll approve of anything that helps us find Gabe."

"May I stay and watch?" I ask, and immediately regret it. If I had just hung around, my mother would have hardly given my presence any thought. But now that I've asked, she has to make a decision about what would be best.

"Don't you have to work?" she asks as she pulls some half-burned candles out of a drawer and arranges them in lumps of clay around the edges of the coffee table.

"Today's my day off. Linda is making Joe give me one day off a week."

My mother shrugs. "Just don't ask any questions. This is Margo's reading."

Ten minutes later Margo and Shawnee arrive simultaneously. Shawnee gives Margo a big hug in our living room and tells her that the whole world feels the pain of a lost child.

"Would anyone like tea?" my mother asks, lighting the candles. Both Shawnee and Margo say no, thank you. Good thing. I don't think we have a tea bag in the house.

Shawnee takes off her man's sweater and sets herself down in the center of the sofa. Margo goes around to the other side of the coffee table and kneels before it. I can tell by her eyes and the way that her hands are shaking that she's nervous. Shawnee hands Margo the cards. "Shuffle the cards while thinking of your question," she says.

Mom and I sit on the floor too, but farther away.

Margo hands the cards back to Shawnee, who draws nine cards and arranges them in rows of three on the table. As she turns them over she says, "My! So many cards from the Major Arcana! The cards have a lot to say to us today." She points to the top three cards. "This is what has happened in the past," she says.

I lean over and look at the three past cards. My mother doesn't seem to mind—she's doing the same thing. There is the Page of Pentacles, the Hermit, and the Five of Wands. "Ah," says Shawnee. "Ah. We have a boy who has been assessing his skill, testing his power. He has been insisting on exercising his own will. However, as the Hermit shows us, power comes from shining the light on and accepting our contradictions. That is a hard task."

Margo nods as if she knows exactly what Shawnee is talking about. But like me, I bet she's eager to hear the present and the future.

"These three cards," says Shawnee, pointing to the middle cards, "tell us about the present." Again we lean over the cards. There are the Lovers, Temperance, and the Moon. I can't wait to hear the story the pictures tell. She begins with the Moon.

"Ah, see how these dogs howl at the moon?" says Shawnee. "Gabe is dealing with overwhelming feelings."

"Then he's alive?" Margo asks, lifting herself off the floor.

Shawnee puts one finger up and closes her eyes. She appears to be listening, as if she and an imaginary friend are having a conversation.

"Yes," says Shawnee. "I'm certain that he is alive."

My mother jumps up and hugs Margo, then kneels, resting her hand on Margo's knee, to listen to Shawnee's reading. Margo keeps wiping tears from her eyes and taking deep breaths. About the present, Shawnee talks again of will, but this time of *true* will. She says true will is knowing who you really are and what you truly need. I remember realizing at Bernadette's last night that I don't know Gabe very well. Have I ever? Does Gabe know himself? Do I know myself? Probably not, I decide.

"In this position," Shawnee tells us, "the Lovers card signifies that with acceptance and an understanding of our true self, love will come."

"And the future?" asks my mother. "Do you have any way of being more specific, Shawnee, about the future?"

Shawnee doesn't answer my mother, but runs her fingers along the bottom three cards. The King of Swords, the World, the Queen of Pentacles.

"Your son has a choice to make." Shawnee points to the middle card, the World. "See this crown around the woman? It is the crown of death or the crown of victory. The choice will be a matter of determining who is to be in control."

"Like father, like son," Margo says.

This startles me. I have never heard Margo talk about Mike and Gabe's relationship before. I wonder, not for the first time, whether Margo knows more about why Gabe is missing than anyone is saying.

"What can I do?" Margo asks.

Again Shawnee closes her eyes and has a silent conversation.

"Nothing," says Shawnee. "This is an internal journey."

"Can you tell us anything about where Gabe *is*?" asks my mother. I can tell she's disappointed—she was hoping for more concrete information.

This time Shawnee keeps her eyes closed for much longer. "He's not in the mountains or in the city," says Shawnee. "I feel him, he's surrounded by water." She opens her eyes and tells us, "Water symbolizes the soul."

My mother takes Margo's hands and tries to remind her of the good things we've heard. He's alive. He's on an internal journey—like a quest. All young men have to go on a quest of one kind or another.

"Look at Billy," says Mom. That's my father. "He's still on his boyhood quest!"

Margo and my mother laugh. Shawnee signals for me to come sit beside her on the couch.

"You have a question you want to ask." She hands me the cards. "Think of your question and then choose one card."

"Do I have to say my question out loud?" I whisper.

She shakes her head no.

I want to ask about Benny, but I feel way too selfish. Certainly, if I ask my silly question while Gabe is missing, the gods will take Benny away from me for good.

Shawnee reads my mind. "It's okay to ask *your* question," she says. "Sometimes the answer to one question is the solution to many."

So I silently ask God, Mother Goddess, the Universe, whomever, *Will Benny come back to me?* and pick a card.

TWENTY-EIGHT

I sit in the rear of the bus after school; Gabe sits in the front.

Once home, I grab a Scooter Pie and come running outside; Gabe stays inside. I make up a question regarding our homework and go knock on his door.

Margo opens the door wide and says, "We have one unhappy boy here."

Gabe, who had been sitting on a radiator near the table, jumps up in fury and bangs upstairs. I saw him just long enough to notice that his eyes are red and his face is blotchy. He's been crying.

"He better cut that out before Dad gets home," says Mary.

"What a sissy-boy," Timmy says.

"Anna broke up with Gabe today, Jocelyn," Margo says to me. "Why don't you go upstairs and see if he'll talk to you."

I'm not sure I like this assignment. I have rarely been welcomed into Gabe's room—a room he shares with both brothers and is at the same time rather barren and entirely male. I knock on the door.

"Go away!" Gabe shouts.

"Can I come in?" I ask. "I have a question about our book reports."

"No."

"I'm sorry about Anna," I say. "I know you really like her."

The door opens a crack, and Gabe turns to fling his body on his bed.

I guess this means I can enter after all. Not much in the room has changed. Two beds. One mattress on the floor. It's easy to assume that one of the beds collapsed under horseplay and was eventually taken out for repair. Two bureaus. A carpet of T-shirts, pants, and socks. I immediately look to the spot on the wall where Anna's letter hung the last time I was in this room. It's held by tacks in each corner but torn in two.

"What did she say?" I try not to let the little trickle of pleasure I feel deep in my belly reach my face. Anna has broken up with Gabe, and I am his consoler. But it doesn't matter what expression I have on my face because Gabe is looking up at the ceiling. He doesn't even bother to turn toward me.

"Her parents found out about us and said that she's too young to date."

I speak the indisputable truth: "Then she still likes you."

"I don't think so," he says. "I think she's just using her parents as an excuse. I think she's sick of me but doesn't want to hurt my feelings."

I see that this could be true too. Anna is known for her kindness. I cautiously sit on the bed across from Gabe's. "Why would she be sick of you?"

Gabe sits up and shrugs. "I'm determined to make her like me again," he says. "I can do it too."

I think of the seminar my mother took one weekend: "The Power of the Mind." She tells me that you can change your life just by focusing your thoughts. I wonder if Gabe somehow already knows about the power of the mind. He certainly seems able to make his life turn out okay.

Then I'm hit by a new thought: What if Gabe uses the power of the mind to make Anna like him again, and I use my thoughts to make Gabe like me? What would happen? I smile.

"You don't believe me, do you?"

"I believe you," I say. "That's why I'm smiling."

TWENTY-NINE

Getting ready for work, I ponder the two things I've been told about Gabe and his disappearance. Bernadette says Gabe is "at confession." Shawnee says Gabe is surrounded by water. Holy water? Gabe *was* last seen coming from the church; and Bernadette told me flat out to ask Father Warren where he is.

I decide to leave early and hang out at Ray's Market at 6:30 a.m.—one half hour before going to the Grill—knowing that Father Warren picks up the *Manchester Union Leader* here every morning. I overheard him say so one day at breakfast.

"Hi, Father Warren," I say as he comes out, and I just seem to be walking by.

"Look at this, Jocelyn," he says. Again I get a small feeling of pleasure from the smile he directs my way. "The Red Sox won another game. Just might go all the way this year."

"Does the paper say anything about Gabe O'Neil?" I ask.

"I haven't seen any mention yet," says Father Warren. "It seems that his disappearance has moved off the front page."

"Not for me," I say. The force of my voice startles me. What have I done so far but be a passive observer?

"Do you know Gabe well?" Father Warren asks as we both begin walking toward the Grill.

"We've known each other forever. He's my next-door neighbor, and we work together at Joe's, you know."

Father Warren stops and turns toward me. "Did he tell you anything, Jocelyn, that might have indicated something was wrong? Did he seem upset by anything in the days before he left?"

I feel embarrassed every time someone asks me this type of question. Gabe and I did see each other at the Grill every weekend during the school year, and of course we ran into each other occasionally in the halls or in our yards. Yet I seem to know so little. But I try to think of the last time I actually had a chance to observe Gabe. It must have been the Sunday morning before the last days of school. The Grill stays open only a few hours on Sundays—to catch the church crowd. Sometimes Joe would ask us to work on Sundays, sometimes not. I'm trying to remember what it was like that morning when suddenly my brain snags on a memory.

"You know," I say with sudden recollection, "Gabe did seem really moody the Sunday before he disappeared."

"What do you mean 'moody'?"

"He was quieter than usual. The regulars were kidding him, insinuating that he had 'partied hearty' the night before. Usually, Gabe just shrugs that off or plays along, but he didn't that morning. He ignored the regulars like he couldn't even hear them."

"Did he say anything, anything at all, Jocelyn, that might have given you a clue as to why he was acting this way?" There is an intensity to Father's voice that makes me realize he's feeling as desperate as everyone else to find Gabe.

"If I remember anything, I'll let someone know," I say as we walk up the steps to the Grill.

"Come to me, Jocelyn," says Father Warren. "If you think of anything at all, please come tell me."

It isn't until later, after I've swept the floor of the Grill, that I realize that I never asked Father Warren what *he* knew.

THIRTY

One late afternoon in August, Gabe brings me to the rickety house in the woods for a second visit. Although little has changed, I am no longer shocked by the interior decorating. Instead, I feel privileged to have an inside view. I glance at the posters more openly and notice that a new one, a picture of some rock stars, is hanging on the wall.

"Led Zeppelin," Gabe tells me reverently. "They're new."

I nod in appreciation.

We hear someone calling Gabe's name and rush outside. I know that Gabe's brothers will kill him if they discover that he brought me here.

The voice grows louder. It is familiar, but I don't recognize it as the voice of Matt or Timmy. Gabe calls back. I follow him away from the sight of the house, and we nearly collide into the caller. It's Gabe's cousin Jay.

"What are you doing here?" Gabe asks.

"My mother is at your mother's dentist," Jay says, as if that explains everything. And for the guys, it does.

I hate this news. I hate this arrival. I hate that Gabe and I no longer have a secret together. I hate that Jay will learn about the house too. I hate that he will expect me to back off and let the real games begin. I hate that Gabe will let it happen.

"So what are you guys doing down here?" Jay asks. He winks at Gabe.

I turn to Gabe to answer. He hesitates. Should he tell Jay about the house? He hasn't made up his mind. I want to prevent it at any cost.

"God, it's hot," I say. "Let's go undie-dipping."

Jay looks at Gabe as if to say, *She's not serious, is she?*

"I'll take my clothes off if you do," Gabe says to me.

I look over at Gabe. We *are* comrades. We are protecting the house. I pull off my shorts and toss them on the bank.

Gabe does the same with his shorts. He takes his shirt off too. Gabe glances over at Jay with that smile in his eyes.

I wade into the water. The August nights have begun to cool off. I raise my arms in response to the chill.

"Jesus," says Jay. Then he seems to change his mind. "Okay," he says, pulling his shorts and T-shirt off. "But," he says to me, "Gabe and I have our shirts off, so you have to take your shirt off too."

They are both staring at my nearly wet T-shirt. I don't want to take it off. I've just started to grow. Will they tease me because I'm starting breasts? Will they tease me because they're not bigger? I pull the shirt away from my body. "No way," I say.

"Come on," says Jay, who is standing along the water's edge facing me. "You were the one who suggested we do this. If you're not going to take your shirt off, then take your underpants off."

I look at Gabe. I rescued him when Jay asked what we were doing. Surely he will rescue me.

Gabe is smiling at Jay. "Take off yours," he says to him. Neither boy is coming into the water.

"Why should I take mine off? I have one piece of clothing on. You have one piece of clothing on. She should have one piece of clothing on too." His voice is serious. Direct.

I want this conversation to end. I think about leaving, but I think that perhaps Jay will leave first, and then Gabe and I will be left to our own adventure. I want Jay to leave. I debate taking something off. My underwear? I'm in the water now. They probably can't see me. But even below my waist I am caught in the middle. I am no longer a girl, but nowhere near a woman. Will they make fun of me because I've begun to grow hair? Will they ridicule me because I have so few? What am I supposed to look like now, anyway?

"You want to see something? I'll show you my bum." It's the only thing I have to offer.

"Oh, big deal," says Jay. "Everyone has an ass. See?" He pulls his underwear down in back and shows me his.

Gabe laughs like this is the funniest thing he has seen in a long time.

"Look, even Gabe has an ass," says Jay.

Right on cue Gabe lowers his underwear and shows me. He waves his back end around.

Things have turned sillier. I flip around and moon the boys. But when I look back, I see that Gabe and Jay have not been looking at me. They have been looking at each other. I hurry out of the water, to get my shorts and go home.

"Where are you going, Jocelyn?" Jay yells. He moves toward me. "Come on. Stay and play."

I soften for a moment. Is he being serious? "What do you want to play?" I ask.

Jay laughs as if this is the funniest thing he's heard. "How about you show me yours and I'll show you mine." Jay looks at Gabe.

"Come on, Joss," says Gabe. "Give him a peek."

"Give him a peek yourself," I say. I see a look of anger or excitement come over Gabe's face—I'm not sure which—but it scares me. I turn and walk quickly down the path.

Without words, Gabe and Jay are racing toward me. I run, but I don't stand a chance. Gabe throws me down. I land facedown in the dirt and pine needles. My legs are scratched by low brush. Gabe rolls me over and sits on my stomach the way he has a hundred times before, only this time he pulls up my shirt. I try to pull it down, but he pins my hands. Jay pulls at my shirt. Then he pulls my pants down around my ankles. I hear words and laughing. Gabe slides off my stomach, but his knees still hold me down. I feel fingers, at first only poking, then pinching and probing. They rub against me, but I am no longer on the bank of Kiddy Brook. I am far away.

Finally, they stop.

Gabe says, "Hey, get up. Get up, Jocelyn!"

"Leave her," says Jay. "She's a whore."

I don't dare get up for a long time after Gabe and Jay leave. I'm afraid that they are hiding along the trail, that they'll jump out of the woods and trap me again. It would be Gabe's way of showing me just what foolish rubbish I am.

I pull down my T-shirt and look for my underpants and shorts. The panties are ripped, so I slip my shorts on without them. Afraid that my mother will see my underpants back home and ask me what happened, I bury them deep in the mud.

How could I explain that I had thought it would be okay to take my clothes off in front of boys? My mother would tell me, as she always does, that I had gotten exactly what I deserved. And I had. It takes a long time to dig a hole deep enough so that no one will ever find this trace of me again.

Dora, a counselor my mother works with, asks me to babysit her four-year-old son, Stone. He and I create many adventures for his bionic man action figure, but they all can be summed up this way: Six Million Dollar Man captures and pulverizes Creepy Bad Guy.

Then we play three games of Chutes and Ladders, read two stories, eat one more bowl of Quisp cereal, and I put him to bed. He calls me back four times before going to sleep.

I call Theresa, raid the kitchen cupboard (which means eating a whole bag of chocolate chips), and watch a scary movie on TV. I try to stay awake through the news, but I'm never successful. When I wake at 1:30 a.m., Dora is still not home.

The news and late-night shows are over. Now there is church. A minister stands in front of enormous bouquets of flowers, wearing a microphone and talking about forgiveness. He suggests that we try putting ourselves in the shoes of another.

I think about that. I think about Benny, who I miss like crazy at this hour, and wonder if I have really tried to see things from his point of view. Maybe I haven't been a very good friend lately. I mean, he's been taught that sex before marriage is a sin. Have I tried to understand this? What would I do if *my* mother were really sick, maybe dying? Could I continue to do things that I know she wouldn't approve of?

Meeting Mrs. Desanctis for the first time was so hard. I mean, it's nerve-racking meeting your boyfriend's mother on any day, but Benny had told me how sick she was, and I've never known how to act around bedridden people.

I remember that I borrowed Mom's car to visit Benny, which already made the day a big deal. I never borrow the car. I hate getting the third degree, so I usually opt for my bike instead. But this one time I didn't want to arrive at the Desanctises' all hot and sweaty. I read somewhere that a person's first impression sticks, and I wanted to make a good one.

I arrived just as Mr. Desanctis was leaving to play golf. He hoisted his clubs into the trunk of his car and said, "So, you're Jocelyn."

I held out my hand like I'd seen boys do in movies. "Hi, Mr. Desanctis," I said.

"It's a pleasure to *finally* meet you," he said. His smile told me that not only did he like me, but Benny did too. I felt stronger going into the house.

Mrs. Desanctis was smaller than I anticipated. Not just thin, that I did expect, but petite. She was sitting up in her bed, dressed in black polyester pants and a baggy T-shirt, trying to do a crossword puzzle. Behind her hung a crucifix.

"What's a four-letter word for 'boring'?"

"Dull?" said Benny, throwing himself on the only chair in the room and patting a knee for me to rest on.

"Get up, Benjamin, and let Jocelyn sit down. Begins with an 'f,'" said his mother.

"That's okay," I said.

"Well, at least come sit on the bed with me."

"Funk?" asked Benny.

"Flat?" I asked, sitting on the very end.

"I know," shouted Benny. "Fred!"

"Benny!" Mrs. Desanctis laughed. Fred is Benny's father's name.

Mrs. Desanctis threw the crossword puzzle down. "Life," she said.

"Now, Ma," said Benny, getting up and moving over to his mother. "Your life isn't boring. Your hair, maybe, but certainly not your life. Not when you have me." He snuggled up to her like an eager puppy.

"How do you put up with this guy, Jocelyn?" asked Mrs. D.

I smiled.

"I'm just so sick of these four walls."

"Would you like to go somewhere?" I asked. I knew that Benny had been left with the truck, but I had the car. I could take us all out.

Mrs. D. and Benny looked at each other as if I'd suggested something criminal.

"Your father would kill us."

"So he'd lecture us for a while. 'What would you have done if your mother needed immediate medical care?' It might be worth it."

"That kind of talk worries me, Benjamin."

"Don't worry, Ma. I only take risks with your life, not mine."

I drove us all to the brand-new Mall of New Hampshire in Manchester. Mrs. D. was like a child who had been let loose at Disney World for the first time. She listened to Benny's favorite records with earphones. "How can you understand the words, Benny?" she said.

"You're right, Ma. 'Mares eat oats and does eat oats' is so much easier to comprehend."

She bought us french fries and ice-cream sundaes at the food court. Then, before leaving, we wandered into a department store that had wigs for sale. Mrs. D. tried on a long-haired wig.

"Barbra Streisand!" said Benny.

I had to laugh.

She tried on a wig that was blond and another that was silver. When she took the silver wig off, Benny leaned over his mother's shoulders and said, "Perfect."

Mrs. Desanctis looked up at her wigless reflection in the mirror.

"I like this one best," said Benny.

Suddenly, I feel terrible. Clearly, all I've thought about is me and what I need. I decide right then and there to do something differently tomorrow. I'll show Benny that I can be a real friend.

During my lunch break I ride my bike over to Mason Florist. They have flowers arranged in baskets and vases shaped as wheelbarrows or baby shoes. The arrangements make me nervous. I guess they remind me of my grandmother's funeral and the bouquets that filled every room of our tiny house.

Fortunately, I see the cut flowers in a refrigerator behind the counter. I remember Benny telling me in May that his mother was grumpy because the tulips take so much longer to come out here in New

Hampshire than in New Jersey. She was partial to tulips, he said. I purchase a bunch of yellow tulips tied up with a pretty blue ribbon.

When I get back to the Grill, I ask Linda if I can keep the flowers in the walk-in, and she agrees. "Just tuck them out of the way, so Joe doesn't see them. You don't need an interrogation from him."

I can't believe how nervous I am when I ride over to Benny's after work. I'm not sure if it's because I've only talked to Mrs. Desanctis a few times or if it's because I don't know how Benny will react to my just showing up. I hope he'll be pleased.

I park my bike on the lawn and knock on the door to the little Cape Cod. I hear Benny telling his terrier, Roadkill, to pipe down. And then I hear him say in an upbeat voice, "I'll be right there!"

When he opens the door, however, his face registers confusion.

"Hi, Benny," I say quickly. "I came—I remembered that your mom likes tulips and thought these might cheer her up."

"Are your friends here, Benny?" It's Mrs. Desanctis calling from the room that used to be a den but is now her bedroom.

"It's Jocelyn, Mom." He nods his head in the direction of her room—his way of inviting me in.

"Look what she brought you," he says. His voice is loud, boisterous.

I worry for a moment that Benny is trying too hard. It occurs to me for the first time that his mother might not want me here. Perhaps she has begun to side with Father Warren, feeling that Benny shouldn't see so much of me. Maybe *she* asked Father Warren to talk to Benny.

"Jocelyn, how wonderful!" says Mrs. Desanctis, pulling herself up. She's tucked in bed with magazines and newspapers all around her. Her hair is thinner now and loosely pulled back away from her face. "I've been asking Benny when I was going to see you again." She looks warmly at her son.

Phew. Mrs. Desanctis still likes me. My stomach muscles relax a little. I smile.

But Benny seems anything but relaxed. He keeps looking at his watch and then smiling at his mother or me in this dopey, distracted way. It isn't long before I get why.

"Hey, Ben, you ready?" I recognize the voice of Tom Eldridge.

"Just a sec, Tom."

"I told some guys that I'd play a pickup game this afternoon," Benny says.

I can't tell if he's torn or if he's a little irritated that I'm upsetting his plans. I'm hoping to put him at ease, to tell him that I understand how awkward I've made everything in the past few weeks. That I'll be understanding. I won't be so selfish.

Benny looks at me and then looks at his mother. Maybe it's permission to leave he's seeking. Or maybe he doesn't trust me to say the right things around his mother when he's gone.

"Go ahead," I say. "I want to tell your mother about life at the Grill these days."

Benny smiles and says, "Okay. See ya." He kisses his mother on the cheek and says, "You two behave." Then he pulls my hair as he leaves.

I know that I did exactly what I set out to do. I was a better friend. So how come it feels *so* bad?

THIRTY TWO

I have not told my mother—or anyone else, for that matter—what happened with Gabe and Jay in the woods. Instead, I keep to myself during the day. It is amazing, if you work at it, how many hours you can go in a day without someone talking to you. I work at this.

At night I crawl into my bed and ask angels to surround me. I picture them flying into my room—all shapes and colors and sizes. I imagine having real conversations with some while the others look on and smile.

I keep the light on for as long as I can. When my eyes get heavy, I give myself a pep talk: *Jocelyn, these are the best hours of the day. You now have eight more hours that are yours and no one else's. No one will tease you or make mean remarks. No one can hurt you.*

It usually gives me a sense of comfort—eight hours is a long time. A long time before I have to worry that my secret will be told.

THIRTY THREE

There is no search party this morning. No dogs, no men in hiking gear. The deafening helicopters that still buzzed over Weaver Falls yesterday have gone home.

Today the Grill is a hangout for kids who knew Gabe in any remote way. They have been brought closer by this trial. They don't want to let go of the heightened feelings that come with a crisis. They don't want to give up the chance that someone from a different side of the lunchroom will speak to them now. So the jocks and cheerleaders tentatively talk to geeks from the Latin club, who have somehow struck up a conversation with the greasers, who put their orders in through me.

I have not met Benny's eyes since he walked into Joe's. Even though I enjoyed talking with his mother, I still feel hurt that he could choose friends over making things right with me. He's sitting with them now, laughing at inane jokes and flirting with some girls who are on their way to hike the mountain.

I'm definitely feeling a little second-class today. Why is it that I'm the only one working? Granted, lots of these kids have jobs that will begin later in the day—like lifeguarding at the town pool or the evening shift at the A & P. But for once I'd like to sit down and have someone take *my* order.

"Didn't I play with you and Gabe when I was little?" a kid says to me while I refill his coffee cup. He's an artist, a kid who loves to draw silly animal characters. They're good. He's sitting with a whole group of kids that I hardly know. Not popular, but not fringe, either.

"I remember that day," I say, feeling my face heat up. And I do. His mother brought him over to Mrs. Cavanaugh's when Gabe and I were there.

"You stole my hat."

Oh, my God, I think. I did. Gabe wasn't happy about this kid hanging out with us, so we sort of ganged up on him. Took a lot of his things. Hid them. "Sorry about that," I say.

"Well, I guess I can forgive you," he says, smiling. He has awesome teeth.

I look over at Benny, who happens to be staring at me.

"I'm Steve," he says, pulling me back.

"Jocelyn," I say.

"Hey, Jocelyn," says a boy at Benny's table. "Are we going to get our toast?"

When I feel like it, I think.

Steve and his friends get up and start digging in their pockets for money. "Maybe we can play together again sometime," Steve says.

"What would we play?" I expect him to say, *Doctor,* in which case I will not know whether he likes me and is flirting with me or suspects I'm an easy lay.

"I play a mean game of Monopoly," he says.

My breath catches.

"Joss," Benny says from behind me.

I look down to see if I need to give Steve change.

"Bye, Joss," says Benny as he heads out the door.

I hardly mind that he's gone.

THIRTY FOUR

We always go to the regional high school basketball tournament with Gabe's family. This year Weaver Falls High is in the finals. Matthew is playing. Timmy and Mary are going with friends. Gabe meets his mother as she gets out of her car. He's in his sneakers, sliding around in the slush. He doesn't see me emptying the trash next to our shed.

"Can I bring a friend tonight?"

"Jocelyn will be there," I hear Margo say as she gathers groceries from the car.

I slide farther behind the shed and hold my breath while waiting to hear Gabe's answer.

"All right," Margo says. "Call Jay. We can pick him up on the way."

Jay? I guess a look said everything. I'm not surprised. Gabe has not talked to me since that day last summer at Kiddy Brook. He doesn't act mad at me—it's not like I told or anything—I've simply ceased to exist. In school he avoids looking at me. Once when our French teacher suggested we work together, Gabe asked to be excused to use the bathroom. He never returned, and Mademoiselle Widely never noticed. The weird thing is: I wasn't relieved. I was disappointed. How is it that you can still miss someone who treats you like "shit on his shoe," as my mother would say?

I slip back into the house, my stomach in knots. Will Jay and Gabe antagonize me the way they did at the brook? I think about not going, but then I realize that Mom and Margo will be in the car. They wouldn't dare.

Later I slide in the backseat of the O'Neils' station wagon with my mother. Gabe sprawls in the way back. I used to ride back there with him, but I'm clearly not invited. We pick up Jay, who joins Gabe in the back (without so much as a glance at me), and head to the University of New Hampshire for the game. Have they forgotten last summer?

I sit next to my mother in the bleachers and glance around for other kids I know. Gabe and Jay are seated behind the basketball team, where they can feel like they're part of the game plan, part of the action. We're seated many rows up—parents, supportive spectators.

Between the boys and the parents, I recognize some girls from my class. Anna is with them. For a moment I contemplate going and sitting on the edge of the group. I wonder if they'd be nice and talk to me. It's been a long time since I've tried to be one of them. Somehow, with church and youth group and invitations behind the cemetery, they've created a whole world that I don't belong to. When I'm around them in school, I feel like there is so much that I don't know. And when I think about what I've done, there is so much that I don't want them to know. I decide to stay where I am.

Every three or four minutes Mike stands up and screams at the ref. His sentences are filled with half-completed words and groans so those around him can fill in the blanks. When he sits back down, he tells Margo and my mother what the coach should be doing to win the game. Margo spends the whole game asking him to calm down.

My mother, on the other hand, has become more excited with every basket Weaver Falls scores. When the game is tied at the end of the first half, she begins jumping up with the other high school kids, shouting along with the cheerleaders.

Cheerleaders: "Carl, Carl, he's our man, if he can't do it . . ."

My mother: "Matthew can!" (My mother knows

that the cheerleader whose turn it is to call out a name is Matthew's girlfriend, so she joins in on the cheer.)

I begin to feel warm and sticky. The other seventh graders, who really don't care about the tournament, keep turning around to see who is shouting from the stands. Each time one of the girls in the group below looks directly at us, my stomach tightens. I contemplate crawling under the bleachers, where surely it would be cooler and less embarrassing.

At the end of the third quarter I hear Samantha Siviski call my name. I look down, and she gestures for me to join the girls. I hesitate. Even though I'm sure she said "Jocelyn," I don't want to be mistaken. Perhaps there is someone behind me whom she's calling.

When two or three girls call my name, I thaw and begin to negotiate my way between laps, feet, and winter coats to the group below.

Samantha moves to the side to make room for me to sit. "Courtney says that you came with Gabe O'Neil and his cousin," she says, demanding to settle the bet.

I nod.

"What did they talk about in the car?"

"Did they mention Anna's name?" asks Courtney. Anna blushes.

I'm dumbfounded. "I don't know," I admit. "They were in the way back of the station wagon. I really couldn't hear what they were saying."

"Didn't you talk with them at all? Even a little?"

I shake my head no.

"You're useless," says Samantha. "Go back to your seat. It's too squishy here."

I make my way back up the bleachers.

For the rest of the game I wonder what I should have said instead. Should I have made something up? Would it have been so hard to say, *I think I did hear the name Anna*? Would that little bit of information have made a place for me until the game ended? The heat, the humiliation, and the smell of my own perfume is beginning to make me nauseous.

Weaver Falls wins the tournament by three points. Gabe and Jay are elated. About halfway home the two of them have exhausted their loud analysis of the game (no talk of Anna here). It's suddenly dead quiet in the back. Then Jay sits up and turns toward the backseat, where my mother and I are sitting.

"What did you think of the game, Jocelyn?"

He sounds sincere. But I don't trust him. "Great," I say, my brain leaping for something, anything else to say that won't provoke teasing. At the same time my stomach makes its final leap to my throat.

"Stop the car please, Mike," I squeak.

"You better stop, Mike," says my mother. "Jocelyn looks horrible."

The car pulls over. I jump out and barf at the side of the road while Gabe and Jay snicker with repulsion from the back.

THIRTY FIVE

Benny's waiting for me when I get off work in the afternoon.

"What are you doing here?" I ask.

"I thought you'd be happy to see me," he says.

Ha! So this is how it's going to be. He doesn't want to be with me, but he doesn't want me to be with anyone else either. *Thank you, Steve,* I think. We banter our way back to the picnic tables. Then Benny's quiet for a moment.

"I think my mom is slipping, Joss. She's sleeping so much more now, and when I talk to her, she just smiles weakly. Like it takes too much energy to talk."

"She's storing her energy, Benny," I say. "She's a fighter. Just like you."

"Lately, I just seem to be losing all the battles."

"What have you lost?" *Please say "you" so I can tell you that you're way off.*

"My sense of fairness."

"Life isn't fair, Benny," I tell him. And I mean it. When I compare my life to the lives of the other girls (except Bernadette), I know that life isn't fair. Not one bit.

"Do you get angry at God, Jocelyn?"

"I do, Benny. And I tell him so."

Benny laughs. Guess he thinks he and God have something in common.

"And what does he say back?"

"I'm not talking about God if you laugh at me."

I scoot up on the picnic table next to him and kick off my Keds. Benny places his fingertip on my leg, on my birthmark that's oval and shaped like a fingerprint. Then he lifts his finger gently.

"Look at the mark you made!" I say. It is an old game.

I want to tell him what I think, but I can't. How can I tell him that I thank God every day for bringing Benny to Weaver Falls? How can I tell him that what is open and genuine and vulnerable in him allows me to see some good in me? That when he loves me, I actually feel like God's on my side. I can't tell him because I can't separate God's feelings from my own feelings.

I just sigh.

Benny takes my hand and begins to play with my

fingers. I look at him, hard. I want him to admit that he wants to be with me. Finally, he speaks.

"Look at my eyes." He turns his whole body toward me. "Have you noticed? Our eyes are identical, Jocelyn. We have the very same eyes."

I feel a tingle from my toes to the tip of my tongue. He has never told me that he loves me, but this is an even more wonderful thing to say. Closer to the feeling that I know. I kiss him. Quick. He kisses me back. Hard.

Benny looks behind him and then turns back. "Want to go down to the river?"

I nod my head. I do.

"Just for ten minutes," he says.

I'm only worth ten minutes? But I follow.

THIRTY-SIX

On the last day of school seventh graders take over the Weaver Falls movie theater at 7:00 p.m. The theater plans for this event and has substituted *Fiddler on the Roof* (which has already come to town) for *Ryan's Daughter.* I overheard Joanne and Courtney in homeroom saying that they wished they were seeing *Ryan's Daughter* instead. Supposedly, there's an amazing love scene.

I'm not sure why I asked my mother to drive me to the theater. I guess I want her to think that I'll be meeting up with friends, joking and sharing secrets like she did when she was in seventh grade. Every now and then she asks me what the girls are like in my class (it's easy to describe them when you have so much time to watch) or who I sit with at lunch. I tell her Anna because she is the one friend I used to have, but in truth I sit in the middle of a table between two groups that ignore me.

There are a lot of kids standing outside the theater. They are waiting for friends to arrive before going in. I quickly wave good-bye to my mom and stand near a group, hoping that she'll think that I, too, have someone I'm waiting for. It's a lot of work to not be someone's disappointment.

As soon as she's left, I pay for a ticket and sit in the balcony of the theater—a place my mother would never choose. This is my one reward for coming.

Apparently, everyone wants the balcony. Kids flock into the seats around me. Samantha and Courtney are here. So is Joanne. So is Gabe. So is Anna. Anna hangs back and therefore has to take the one empty seat beside me.

No one is watching the movie. Everyone has seen it before. "Let's play truth or dare," says Samantha.

Before long everyone is clustered together. Some kids are sitting two to a seat; others are actually sitting on the floor facing friends instead of the screen. I can't believe my own bravery. "May I play?" I ask Anna.

Anna pretends not to hear me at first, so I repeat my question.

"Is it okay if Jocelyn plays?" asks Anna.

No one says no, so she shrugs and backs up on her seat to make room for me in the circle.

Paul goes first. He chooses truth.

"Who do you like?" Samantha asks. The group titters.

"My mother," says Paul.

"That's sick," says someone.

"What? You don't like your mother?" Paul asks. "What kind of son are you?"

The game goes on for some time. I'm playing, but not really. No one calls on me to say truth or dare. Kids start to get bored and up the ante.

It's Gabe's turn. He chooses dare. I could have told you that. Gabe will always take a dare.

"Touch a girl's booby," says Mark.

"Whose?" says Gabe, smiling.

All of the girls look at Mark with an expression that says, *If you choose me, I will make your life a living hell.*

He realizes his error. "Jocelyn's," he says.

Gabe doesn't look at me. He just rolls his head back in a grimace of pain that even I can detect several seats away in this barely lit balcony. "No way," says Gabe.

I'm not sure if I feel rejected or protected. *Maybe,* I think, *Gabe is trying not to hurt me again.*

"You have to, O'Neil. It's a dare."

Anna talks to the girl next to her, pretending not to be a part of the game.

"No, I don't," says Gabe.

"Then you're out of the game," says Mark.

"Chicken," says another.

"I don't have to because I already did," says Gabe.

"What? When? No sir."

"Yes sir," says Gabe.

So this is how it will be told. I get up and head to the bathroom, no doubt making my final ruin even easier.

THIRTY SEVEN

Green shadows have begun to fall across the river. It's been longer than ten minutes.

At first Benny is sweet and gentle, then he's rough, consuming. I don't know if he is loving me or eating me alive. I use my lips. I try to slow him down. I resist his pushing me this way and that, but it only makes him love me more forcefully.

Look at me, Benny. Look at me. But he can't. He has lost control and is angry that he has lost control.

Finally, he is quiet. He rests his head on my shoulder. There are tears in his eyes.

A dam has broken, I think, and grief for his mother flows through. I run my fingers through his hair. But he is annoyed by this gesture. He gets up and paces the riverbank.

I feel guilty. I should have made things easier for him, not more difficult. I should have said no. I try to get him to talk to me. "What do the doctors say, Benny?"

He stares at me as if he hasn't heard a word of my question. "This is the last time we can be together, Jocelyn. The very last time."

I feel the punch, but I understand. "You feel like you've betrayed your mother?"

"My mother? I've betrayed not only my mother, I've betrayed God." He picks up a rock and flings it into the river. "I am so weak, Jocelyn, I've betrayed myself."

"And what about me?" I whisper. I know that this is amazingly selfish. Benny's mother is dying, maybe his faith. How can I ask about me? But . . . Benny must feel something for me. He must. Doesn't love count for anything?

"What about you?" he asks. "Do you feel cheap?"

"Cheap?"

"Maybe you don't. You don't have Father Warren asking you every chance he gets: 'What do you think when you're with Jocelyn? Do you touch her? Where do you touch her?'"

"He asks you *where* you touch me?"

"Of course. He's a priest. That's his job."

"And what do you tell him?"

"I tell him the truth. What do you think I tell him?"

"And what does he say?"

"He tells me that you are not of God. You are temptation. God has his angels and his demons, and you are a demon, Jocelyn. You are in partnership with the devil."

My arms are gone. So are my legs. I am barely a wisp of a soul floating along, listening to these words. "And you believe him?"

"I don't know what to believe." He lowers his shoulders and touches one hand to his chin. "You give it away, Jocelyn."

I give it away. Benny wouldn't sin if I didn't give it away.

THIRTY-EIGHT

The restroom of the movie theater is a filthy, dismal place. I splash cold water on my face and try to decide what to do. I could wait outside for my mother to pick me up, but the movie is a long one and I'd be out on the sidewalk for over an hour. I could beg the box-office attendant to let me call her, but I'm too upset to fake sickness and I can't possibly handle her questions.

I decide to go into the main part of the theater in hopes of an empty seat. I find one in the back, next to a girl my age. I glance over as I sit down. The girl has long hair and is wearing moccasins. I know, because she is sitting cross-legged. She isn't watching the movie. She's reading *Wuthering Heights*.

For the second time today I can't stop myself from doing a bold thing.

"I love that book," I say. It's true. I have read about

a gazillion books this year: *Little Women, The Exorcist, Joy in the Morning,* but my favorite is *Wuthering Heights.*

"Don't you feel so sorry for Heathcliff?" the girl asks.

"Yes. And I wish Cathy had chosen him instead."

"Except that it would be so typical—"

"Shhh!" The older couple behind us are probably the only ones in this noisy theater actually watching the movie.

I wait a few minutes, lean over, and whisper, "How can you read in the dark?"

"I've already read it," she says. "I'm just sort of skimming when the light gets brighter."

I sit back, fascinated by this girl. Where have I seen her before?

She looks up to find me staring at her. "I'm new to the seventh grade," she says. "And I've already seen this movie twice. Do you want to go outside and talk?"

When my mother comes, Theresa and I are sitting on the sidewalk talking about characters in books as if they were our true friends and acquaintances. If Gabe and the others left the theater, I didn't see them.

When I tell my mother about Theresa, she asks, "What about Anna?"

"Oh, Theresa is so much deeper," I say.

"Don't be mean," says my mother.

THIRTY-NINE

I call in sick the next day. Joe flips out on the phone, reminding me that Gabe is gone and that I can't take a day off.

I figure it's Joe's restaurant. He could close the Grill a day in honor of Gabe. Besides, it's Sunday. The Grill is only open a few hours. "I'm sorry," I tell Joe. "I'm sick. I'm not coming in."

Mom heads out to a prayer circle. I pour myself a glass of orange juice and go back up to bed. I lay there, curled up in a ball, frozen for a long time. After what seems like hours, I don't feel agitated. I don't feel anything.

I listen for my breath. I can't hear it, but I can feel it flowing in and out. Gently. I think of the word *gently,* and it makes me cry.

That's how the tears start. Gently. But then they

come faster and faster, and I can't keep my breath even. I scream. I gulp. I sob.

I get up and walk circles on my braided rug. I think of calling Benny. I think of telling him that he *has* to meet me—that he has to help me sort this out. But I'm so afraid of hearing more. All I can think of is Father Warren's words: *She is not of God.*

Am I of God? Or is there something about me that others instinctively know is not good or worthy? What makes me so contemptible? Am I truly Evil Girl?

It was only a few days ago that I talked with Father Warren on the street. (I cringe now when I think of Benny telling this man where he's touched me.) Does this priest, the very one who told me to come to him if I had any thoughts about Gabe, really think that I'm Satan?

There is only one person who can give me a direct answer. I get up and throw on some clothes. I try to run a brush through my tangled hair. I wait until I'm certain that church is over, then I hop on my bike and head to St. Mary's rectory.

My knees are shaking as I knock on Father Warren's door, but I have no choice. All these years I've circled around people like a stray dog wanting to find its way into the pack. At some point even the sorriest dog is going to do something that gives him his admission—or not. So here I am. He can call me the devil, or he can welcome me in. Either way, he's got to do it to my face. Then I will know.

A woman comes to the door and tells me that Father Warren is not home. She believes he's still in the sanctuary.

I cross the road and enter the church. It's dark and quiet. The heavy door slams behind me. I look at the holy water but don't dare touch it. I have second thoughts in the vestibule. Do I turn back now?

"Yes? Is someone there?" I hear.

Father Warren comes out of a small room to the left.

"It's me, Father Warren. Jocelyn McGuire."

"Yes, Jocelyn," he says, slowing down. "Come in, come in. Is there something that you thought of? Something that might help Gabe?"

He seems so eager. "I don't have any information regarding Gabe," I say, "but I was wondering if I could talk to you about something else."

Father Warren nods his head. He's disappointed. "Of course." He motions me into the little room, sits at a small desk, and points me into the other chair. "What is it you are wondering about, Jocelyn?"

"It's about me and Benny."

"Go on," he says, as if I'm making him guess.

"Benny tells me that you think I'm in partnership

161

with the devil," I blurt. I don't mean to be so abrupt, but I'm desperate to be clear. To stop hurting.

He looks down and rubs his hands along his lap. "Is this what you came to talk about?"

I nod my head and wait for his reply.

"Jocelyn," he begins.

And I breathe. *Please tell me that God knows me. That I'm not a stranger.*

"If you and Benny are having difficulties, we can schedule a time for the three of us to meet. We could sit down and talk together—um, relationship counseling, if you will." His voice is calmer, controlled, but not the easygoing voice I heard the morning we walked together.

I don't get it. Why doesn't he answer my question? My head is spinning. Was Benny lying? Is *he* the one who thinks I'm nothing more than temptation? Perhaps he's simply making Father Warren the fall guy.

Then I remember that priests have to keep their conversations with their parishioners confidential. Maybe Father Warren feels that he can't talk with me.

"Do *you* think I'm wicked, Father Warren?" *Is my soul really stained?* I hear my seven-year-old self asking. I feel as if my whole life has begged for this answer.

His mouth twitches into an almost smile. Then the door of the church opens again, sending a shaft of light into the little room. Father Warren stands, and without saying a word, he leaves to see who else has entered. He shuts the door of the little room, blocking my view and the view of the other.

I hear a familiar male voice. The two talk in hushed tones, which makes me crazy. Is it Benny? Should I go see? I start to pace around the little room, looking at the altar robes in an open closet, a picture of the Last Supper hanging on the wall, a prayer book open on Father Warren's desk, when something memorable catches my eye. Partially tucked under the book is a faded photograph of Gabe—one that I've seen before. I slide it out to take a closer look. It's a picture of Gabe standing on the dock with his brothers. I wonder if Father Warren uses the picture to show rescue workers what Gabe looks like. But the picture is old; certainly, there are newer ones available. Gabe had his picture taken every other day for one championship event or another.

Matthew and Timmy look handsome, but bored, as usual. Not Gabe. He's staring at the camera as if daring it to take his picture. His shirt is off, his body is tan, his eyes are sparkling. Where have I seen this before?

My breath rushes in. I know exactly where I saw this picture. It was over the door of the rickety house.

The very house that I have wished to erase from my memory.

Someone must have gathered the belongings that were stored in that house. But when? Soon after I was left in the woods nearby? A year later? Two? The picture is fairly weathered. Is it possible that Gabe gave this picture to Father Warren? If so, recently?

I hear Father Warren saying good-bye to the person in the vestibule and, on impulse, tuck the photo into the pocket of my shorts.

"Now then, where did we leave off?" says Father Warren as he slides back into his seat. "Ah, yes. You and Benny."

Time stops. It's as if I wake up from a dream. I clear the sleepies from my eyes and realize one simple fact: This man, priest or not, is not going to answer my question. He does not care about me. He doesn't care if I am the Virgin Mary or Satan himself.

Father Warren rattles on about how adolescence is a confusing time. And I think, *So what do you have to gain from your repeated talks with Benny? Why do you ask him, "Where do you touch her?"*

Suddenly, I feel a little queasy. I get up, mutter some sort of thank-you, and leave.

I park my bike next to our shed and wonder, *Does Father Warren enjoy imagining touching me? Or Benny?*

FORTY

Eighth grade. Theresa and I stay after school to do research on the Second World War. It's April, and our social studies teacher is beginning to get panicky. U.S. history, she says, never gets taught beyond that war. She's determined to take us right up to Vietnam.

After about an hour of taking notes, we've had enough. We head outside early to wait for Theresa's mom to pick us up. There is still snow in patches on the ground, but the sun is bright, the air smells of thawing earth, and the front steps feel warm underneath us.

"Have you signed up yet for the walkathon?" Theresa asks me. Theresa belongs to the outing club, and they're organizing a trash-pick-up walk from Weaver Falls to Milford. If she's not picking up trash, she's protesting the nuclear plant they're building in Seabrook or marching for the equal rights amendment.

I'm about to tell her that I haven't yet but that I will, when a snowball, or should I say *slush ball,* comes flying toward us. Ice and mud splash at our feet. We jump up and bolt into the entryway of the school.

We peer out the tall windows. "Look," I say. "Gabe O'Neil and his friends are across the street."

"Do you think Gabe threw it?" Theresa asked. "Why would he do that?"

I am reminded of Gabe's antics when I used to bring Anna home. "Maybe he likes you," I say.

"Gabe O'Neil?" Theresa cautiously opens the door. She leads the way back onto the front steps. "Why would Gabe O'Neil like me? I'm not his type at all."

"Who is Gabe's type?" I ask. At that moment a small bird decides to inhabit my chest.

Theresa turns to stare at me. "Of course," she says. "How could I not see it? You like Gabe O'Neil!"

"I don't," I say with as much force as I can. I sit down on the steps and throw my head back with my eyes closed. End of conversation.

"The lady doth protest too much, me thinks."

"What does that mean?" I ask.

"It's from Shakespeare. It means that you are trying too hard to convince me, so there must be some truth to what I'm saying."

At that moment another snowball hits me in the arm.

"Come on!" Theresa yells, and we race down the hill toward town. The boys follow, pelting ice. We hide behind the parish house, and then Theresa quietly leads us into the church.

"Should we be in here?" I ask.

"Sure, that's why they keep it open. So you can come in and pray anytime."

I sit in one of the pews and take a deep breath. The air is a musty mixture of candles, smoke, and wood.

"Come see what I found, Joss," Theresa calls from the front of the church. She's behind a small partition and has opened a box of papery wafers. "They're the Communion hosts," she says. She pulls one out and pops it in her mouth.

"You can't do that!" I cry.

"Why not?"

"Aren't they holy? Aren't you eating the body of Christ?"

"Not yet," says Theresa. "They haven't been consecrated by the priest."

"So what are they now?" I ask.

"I don't know, yucky tasting. Try one."

I take one, but I don't put it in my mouth.

"They don't taste *that* bad," says Theresa.

I ignore her and walk to the back of the church to be alone. I stand in front of a statue of the Virgin Mary, trying to remember a prayer. A prayer of forgiveness for all the ways in which I'm not tolerable. No words come to mind, but I think of a song I heard on the radio and sing it softly. When I get to the words *Sweet Jesus come and teach to me your song,* a bubble rises up from inside of me. I place the host on my tongue. It expands as it melts, and I imagine that consecrated or not, I am filled with something holy. I have made my First Communion.

Theresa is still holding the box when she comes back and sees me smiling.

"Want another one?" she asks.

I do.

That night I turn on the TV to watch my favorite Western show. My mother mixes herself a stinger and comes to sit next to me on the couch. I like it when she does that. It usually means that she'll loosen up, talk to me like a friend—that I'll learn something. I let her sip her drink and relax for a few minutes. I think of Gabe and the snowballs, and then during a commercial I ask, "What was my father like?"

"Oh, honey." She sighs, swirling the ice cubes in her glass. "You don't really want me to talk about him."

I look over at her face, which is not cold and tight, but kind. And instantly, I get it. She's right. I don't want to talk about him. If she tells me wonderful things about my father, I will wonder why such a good person would not want to know me, his daughter. If she tells me bad things, I will wonder why there is this buried place in my heart that still loves my father and wishes he would come home.

The show comes back on, and my mother and I watch in silence. I guess that I *have* learned something. In real life you can't always tell the good guys from the bad guys. I sure can't.

After my "little session" with Father Warren, there are two things I'm dying to do. I want to test out my theory on Benny—tell him that I think Father Warren might be some sort of pervert. I wonder if anything would have happened if I'd stayed in that little room.

The other thing I want to do is see if that rickety house is still standing. I make a peanut butter and jelly sandwich and tell myself that I'm being ridiculous. Gabe could not be as close as that shed in the woods. He would have heard the helicopters and known that the whole town was searching for him. And speaking of searching, wouldn't someone, Matthew or Timmy, have thought of looking at the house site? I'm sure they did.

I pick up the phone to call Benny. I dial his number but bang the receiver down before it rings. I don't want to talk to him. No matter what has been happening, it doesn't change what he said to me. *You give it away, Jocelyn.* I wipe off the counter, toss the crumbs into the sink, and head out the door. I can't help myself.

The path looks regularly trodden, and I feel a sting of resentment. Who's been coming here? Silly, I guess, to believe that we'd be the only kids who ever discovered Kiddy Brook. Other children have no doubt come to build rafts and splash like otters in the stream. Perhaps they found the rickety house and have taken it over as their own.

The house startles me. It's smaller than I remember and partially sunk in the mud. One of the corners is falling down. I feel as if I'm visiting a grave, and perhaps I am.

I push open the barely hinged door. Not a whole lot has changed inside. Naked women still adorn the walls, only now they have dart holes all over their bodies. The floor is littered with cans of different sorts: tuna, spaghetti, beer. Apparently, this house lasted from Matthew's to Gabe's party days.

I crouch and pick up a wine bottle. It isn't the slightest bit weathered.

"I wondered when you'd come," says a voice behind me.

I turn and see Gabe standing in the doorway. I

feel like I'm looking at a ghost. I want to run as fast as my Keds will carry me.

"Say something," he says. I doubt that he's slept this week. There are bags under his eyes, and he looks at me as though in a haze. I wonder if he's tripping.

"What should I say?"

"How about, 'You're alive.'"

"You're alive," I parrot. And then I see that he doesn't have any of the normal Gabe bravado. He's hurting in a way that I've never seen Gabe hurt before. I relax a little and say the truth. "I knew you were alive."

He takes a step closer. "Yeah, sure. How?"

I try to figure it out. I decide to be honest. "Because I have watched you and listened to you for so long, Gabe O'Neil, I can feel your breath inside of me. I would know if you were gone."

"You are so fucking weird, Jocelyn."

I feel like slapping him. "Why did you disappear?"

He doesn't like the closeness of this conversation, so he bangs open the door and takes it outside.

"Your family is crazed out of their minds!" I shout, following him. "Whatever you're going through, I'm sure they'd appreciate knowing rather than thinking you're dead."

"You don't know shit."

"I know more than you think, Gabe."

"Yeah, Jocelyn, what do you know?" Gabe sits down on a fallen tree like he couldn't care less what I have to say.

I pace, trying to siphon what I really feel. "I know that you are not the kid you pretend to be."

"Are any of us?" he asks, chuckling in this deranged sort of way. "What makes you think *that*?"

"Well, I've talked to Bernadette, for one thing."

Gabe jumps up as if a bee stung him. "What has Bernadette said?" he demands to know. He runs his hands through his messed-up hair. His face is panicked—a look I've never seen on him before.

I realize at this moment who Bernadette is. Bernadette is the keeper of Gabe's secrets. She's the one he trusts.

"What I mean to say"—choosing my words carefully to protect her—"is that I went to Bernadette's house. I talked with her; she's nice. But she's different from what I thought, from what we all thought."

"Whose fault is that?" asks Gabe.

He's right. But I also know that despite Gabe's ability to turn the tables, something is terribly wrong. "Why are you hiding here, Gabe?" I ask.

He steps away in disgust, as if he had momentarily forgotten what was wrong and now I was insisting on bringing it all back.

I pull the picture out of my pocket and hold it

out for him to see. "I found this in Father Warren's office," I say.

He glances over and then begins to walk in small circles. "So?"

"So it made me remember this house. This picture used to hang above the door."

"I gave it to him, okay?" He won't stand still.

"Why? Why would you give him *this* picture? And why were you seen leaving the church the night you disappeared?"

"What are you asking, Jocelyn?" He stops turning and puts his face in mine. "Do you know that I spend nights with Father Warren at the parish house? Do you feel my breath inside of you when the two of us are getting it on?"

Gabe's aim is perfect. I feel the weight of what he tells me in the center of my gut. He tries to hold back his emotions, but he can't. Tears roll down his face.

"He's why you disappeared."

"No shit, Sherlock," Gabe says, words mixing with an eerie laugh. "The last time I was with him, I just freaked. I couldn't handle it anymore. He would make me do things I didn't expect. It was totally out of my control." He crouches down, his head on his lap.

The pain spreads out to all of my organs, all of my limbs. I can't think of Gabe, so I think of Benny. I think of all the times he's felt forced to ride with Father Warren, forced to answer his questions just so Father Warren can create more pictures—real or imagined—for his collection. How dare that man say I'm evil! How dare he say that I am in partnership with the devil! He is the devil himself!

Without thinking, I place my hand on the back of Gabe's neck.

He looks up at me as if I had just walked into our American history class and done the same thing. "What do you think you're doing?"

I take my hand away.

"What, are you comin' on to me?" He pops back up. "You want to show me that I still have a thing for girls? Okay, Jocelyn, let's go undie-dipping," he says, pulling on his fly.

We're both standing now. I just glare at him. And I get it. For the first time I'm really clear about who the jerk is here.

He's not put off by my stare. He keeps goading. "What is it with you, Jocelyn? How is it that you can still love me?" He reaches out and squeezes my cheeks between his hands. "And you know you do."

It is not a kind gesture, and I snap my face to the side to break free. "Because I blamed myself for all your mean and hateful behavior," I say. "I thought that I made you do those things because I was too stupid, too naïve. I thought that somehow I had asked for it."

He starts to walk away. I run ahead and block him, my face in his. "But I didn't!" I scream. "I didn't ask for it. And it's your shame, Gabe O'Neil—not mine!"

I expect him to haul off and hit me the way his father hits him, but he doesn't. His face becomes calm, his body depleted. He looks at me in the same way he did when we were four and hiding in the bushes. "You're right," he whispers. "It wasn't you. It *was* me."

He grips a tree and moans into it. He's sobbing. This time I don't touch him. I just stand nearby. I want to rush in and fill the very deep, empty place in him, but I know it's impossible.

What Gabe is enduring is too big for me to handle. "Gabe, I'm going to get help," I tell him.

"No. Please don't, Jocelyn." He reaches his arm out to mine. It's as if he's trying to grab me and is begging me at the same time.

I walk over and hug him. At first he stands there rigidly. But I don't back away, and eventually, he folds himself into me.

"I need food," he says. "Can you go back and get me food?"

"Then we'll talk about what to do?"

He nods his head.

"I'll be back," I say.

"Alone?"

"Yes."

"Promise?"

"Promise."

FORTY TWO

I'm sitting on a stool in chemistry, leaning against the lab table listening to Mr. Godin drone on about the fact that mass cannot be created or destroyed. My mother says that our thoughts are an energy that creates our reality. I am using my brain to will this disorganized, ragbag of a teacher to leave the speech and get on with his demonstration.

I'm doing well in chemistry as well as in my other classes. High school teachers love any evidence of a warm body. And I'm less hung up on what other kids think of me now. I like spending time with Theresa, I like my new job waitressing at Joe's on weekends, and I like feeling that I can pull top grades if I want to.

So I pay little attention to the new boy from New Jersey beside me. He's taken the only empty seat in the room, but my prediction is that he won't sit there for long. Samantha Siviski has her eye on him.

I couldn't help but overhear her say in the cafeteria that she would definitely consider going to the Valentine's dance with the new boy if he asked her. Within the week, New Boy will be sitting in the middle of the room with Samantha and friends, bumping the more quiet and studious Perry Jackson to the front with me. (Sorry, Perry.) I knew that talking with this kid would only prompt Samantha to speed up her effort to provide him with a clearer picture of the pecking order (Desirable Friends 101) here at Weaver Falls.

I'm stunned, then, when Samantha tells this new kid, this Benny, that Courtney is absent today and that he's welcome to her seat in the middle of the room if he wants it. "No thanks," says new kid Benny. "I can see Godin's zany drawings better if I sit here."

I look over to see if I've misjudged this guy. Maybe he's a fellow fringe; maybe he's a brainy chemist who *chooses* to sit in the front of the room. Benny looks up at me and smiles.

My curiosity swells like a hydrogen balloon. I find myself turning into Calculating Soap Opera Spy. I can't help myself. I look for his name on activity lists. I eavesdrop on conversations. I follow him in the halls. What classes does he take? Where does he go during his free period? Has he made any friends? Does he play any sports? By the end of a week of spying all I know is that he's an honor student, he's considering trying out for the baseball team, and he's shy. Seems like he would have been a sure yes on the Samantha invitation.

He's absent one day, and I realize that I'm incredibly disappointed. Spying on Benny has become my principal diversion. The next day he returns, and my heart does a wild, primal dance.

When Godin begins to set up an experiment, Benny leans toward me. "Jocelyn, may I see your notes from yesterday?" he asks.

I slide my notebook over, all the while silently repeating the sound of my name from his mouth. Of course he would know my name. He's heard Godin use it half a dozen times. But the fact that he chooses to use it, like we're lab friends or something, puts my poor heart into another thumping spin.

Benny laughs a kindly laugh. "Your notes look like hieroglyphs. Tell me what they say," he says.

I laugh too and whisper my notes aloud, making them sound like poetry.

FORTY THREE

I return to Gabe with leftover fried chicken and potato salad—food that was dropped off at the O'Neils' house but couldn't fit in the overflowing refrigerator and so got crammed into ours.

Gabe is calmer. And ravenous. "I swore that I'd never become like my old man, Jocelyn." He bites into the meat, tears the chicken off the bone. "But I know that deep down, I'm as fucked up as he is."

"You're not your father," I say, watching him eat.

"Yes, I am. Look at me. All you've ever wanted is to be with me, and look how I treated you."

"You didn't have to be with me. That was your prerogative."

Gabe stares inside the thermos of milk I brought him—as if it held the answers. "You scared me, Jocelyn. You seemed to like me so much. But I guess I've always known that there is something off about me, and I wanted you to see it too."

"I wish you could have just told me," I say, and we both laugh.

"You've got to come home, Gabe."

"I can't, Jocelyn. I can't ever come home."

"Of course you can."

"Sure. After a week of hiding out in the woods— so that everyone in this county is looking for me, wondering what has happened—I come sauntering back to say, what? That I got freaked out because I've been screwing my priest?"

"I think people will be sympathetic. Warren's the adult here."

"Ha!" he shouts, and suddenly his force has come back. "Jocelyn, you *don't* know shit."

"There's no—"

"Let me set you straight, Joss. This is my fault. I *wanted* to be with Father Warren. He was always so damn happy to see me. He would talk with me for hours, and he really cared about what was going on in my head. I wanted him to invent reasons for me to come to the parish house. Don't you get it, Jocelyn? It's my fault that he got turned on. I made it happen."

"That's just your problem, Gabe. You think you're

in charge. But you weren't the puppeteer here, Gabe. He was. He's a priest! You should hear what he's been saying to Benny. And I probably don't even know the half of it."

"Benny?" says Gabe. "I thought, maybe." But this information doesn't seem to release him, it only makes him more depressed. He sets his cup down and lies back on the riverbank, looking up at the first stars.

I lie back too and rack my brain for some angle that will convince him that coming home will work out.

"Matthew and Timmy were here," he says.

I bolt back up. "They know?"

"No. I hid out in the woods until they searched the house. Then I moved in."

I register a tiny pang of pleasure. He didn't hide from me.

"Jocelyn," he says, "don't you see? I can't come home. No matter what I told them—even if I made something up—they wouldn't be satisfied. There would be endless questions that I can't answer. I know, I've gone through all the possibilities."

"You could tell the truth," I say.

"Do you know what that would do to my family?" Gabe asks. "My father can't deal with this. He'll call me a fucking fag. He thinks homos should be burned at the stake. He'll disown me."

It's amazing. I think, *No matter how some people treat us, we still want their love.*

"And he'll blame my mother," Gabe says. "He'll blame her softness and the way she puts all her faith in the Church. He'll say she pushed me toward Father Warren." He fiddles with a little cross at his throat, hanging from a piece of rawhide. Mine?

"You're strong, Gabe," I say. "You can get through this. Your family will be so glad you're alive that—"

He sighs. "Don't be so sure, Jocelyn. Who would you rather have living under your roof? An accomplished athlete, a good Catholic boy who, perhaps, died tragically? Or some kind of deviant who you don't even really know?"

"I would rather have *you*, Gabe."

Gabe rolls over and lowers his head to my shoulder. I wrap my arms around him, and we both cry.

It's hard leaving Gabe, but I don't know what else to do. I can't hide out with him. He won't come home.

"Will you be warm enough tonight?" I ask. There's a breeze coming off the mountains.

He nods.

"I'll be back first thing in the morning."

"Promise me again, Jocelyn. You won't tell anyone? That's the deal, right? I'm trusting you."

"Yes," I say, pushing away the knowledge that this

is wrong. It is so very wrong to keep this secret from the people who love him. But one more day might help us both to come up with a real solution. "Don't forget that you made a promise to me, Gabe," I add.

He nods. He looks so tired. He's going to sleep tonight, I think.

"Okay, then," I say, but I don't move down the path. "Good-bye."

Gabe leans over and places his lips ever so lightly on mine.

"Good-bye, Joss," he says.

FORTY FOUR

After our third date Benny asks me if I would like to go out to Headlock Pond. He is asking permission to go parking, I think, and against the better judgment of Theresa ("You don't want him to think you're easy"), I nod yes.

When we get to the pond, however, he turns off the car and comes around to open my door. "I love this place," he says, taking my hand and leading me down to the moonlit clearing.

"You do?" I have seen Headlock only on the most scorching days of summer, when it's crowded with families.

"Yeah, I remember the day that Mom discovered it. She couldn't wait to show us. And it was so, I don't know, beautiful—it was like an omen, telling us that the move to New Hampshire was the right thing to do."

The cold air clings to my cheeks, but I have never felt warmer. We step onto the ice, which makes a distant moaning sound. I stop, paralyzed.

"Don't worry," says Benny. "The lake always talks beneath the ice. But it's been frozen solid for a month."

I shiver, and he stops to warm both my hands between his.

"Look up."

I do. Tonight the sky is a well-loved quilt, threadbare holes allowing light in from other universes.

"How does that sky make you feel?" Benny asks.

"Small—tiny, in fact. But somehow significant."

"Exactly," Benny says, wrapping his arms around me.

I smile. I've just received an A on the test. "What do you think that feeling is?" I ask. My mother would tell me that it's our memory—a memory that we've forgotten—that we are connected to all things.

"I've gone to church all my life," says Benny, "and in there I always feel inadequate. Like I'm never measuring up to the person God—or my parents— would want me to be. But out here I can *feel* God. Like he's watching, like he's on my side."

And you brought me here, I think. I want to tell him that I know exactly what he means. That I, too, have experienced that feeling. The feeling that one is ultimately safe and protected—even if it does not seem to be so in this world. But suddenly, I'm shy. Because one of the times that I remember knowing this, knowing this without a doubt, was when I was little and kicking my Mary Janes in church.

FORTY-FIVE

I rehearse what I'm going to say to Gabe as I walk down the path. I'll suggest that we find a way for him to get to one of his brother's or his sister's home. He can hang out there, away from the press, until he's had a chance to talk with his family. I've counted up my tip money, and I'm sure I have enough for him to take a bus to Boston. Theresa could take him to the station in Jefferson.

Gabe isn't outside when I arrive. *Let him sleep,* I think, but I can't.

My knock against the flimsy door makes more of a squeaking, tapping noise than a rap. Not a sound in return. No answer on the second knock either, and my whole body, limb by limb, turns to stone.

The door creaks open with a push. No Gabe.

The cans, wrappers, and tattered magazines that had been scattered two days before are now piled in the corner. Bile (or is it simply disguised hurt?) rises in my throat. I can't help feeling tossed upon this heap.

I dig through the rubble to find clues, a note, a picture drawn in the dirt. Did he leave me nothing? As I lift one of the cans I hear a clinking sound and investigate. Discarded with the trash is the gold cross.

FORTY SIX

"Well, that's sexy," says my mother when I come downstairs in my prom dress. She's being sarcastic. I'm wearing what she would call a granny dress, but so is every other girl this year. We've all chosen Gunne Sax dresses, and I think they're romantic.

I'm not sure my mother ever believed in romance. If she did, she doesn't now.

The dress has lace that begins at my thumbs, climbs up my arms, and cradles my neck. A ribbon ties up the bodice.

As Benny leads me to his car, I tell him my mother's comment.

"Not sexy?" he says. "She has no imagination."

I laugh. "Good thing, I guess."

Benny smiles. We both know that this is a special night.

The prom is held at the ballroom of the King Grant's Inn in Keene. It's the first time the prom hasn't been in the school gym.

Neither Benny nor I can dance, but we pretend, and the night feels magical. So magical, I imagine for a minute that I might be chosen as princess in the royal court. Theresa, Benny, and I are sitting at a table, waiting for girls to be elected.

It doesn't happen. Benny squeezes my hand as if to say, *That's not important. Not tonight.* I smile at him— a knowing smile. When I look up, Gabe has left Bernadette with friends and is walking right toward me.

"Hi, Theresa, Benny."

"Hey, Gabe," says Benny, looking up.

Gabe leans over and gives me a kiss on the cheek. "Joss," he says, then walks away.

"What was that?" asks Benny.

I shrug.

"Cattle branding," Theresa mutters under her breath.

I lift the cross from the rubble and tie the rawhide around my own neck. My anger toward Gabe melts. Into melancholy. When would I get it? It was never about me. Never.

The soft earth springs up, supporting my steps as I head back home. I avoid the roots winding across the path, having traveled here too often to be tripped up any longer. When I reach the road, I see a figure coming out of the O'Neils' gate.

Father Warren.

I'll just look down, I think, pretending that I don't see him walking back toward town, but he spends so much time trying to be visible—throwing back his shoulders, putting on his "I've just visited the poor O'Neil family" airs—that I am forced to walk past him.

"Why, Jocelyn!"

I begin to shake, but my mouth, which has been well trained at the Grill, creeps into a perverse smile.

"Jocelyn, is something wrong?" His eyes meet mine for only a second and then rest upon my neck. "You're—you're wearing Gabe's cross."

"No," I say. "It belongs to me."

"But," he says, clearly grappling with images in his own mind, "Gabe was wearing it—"

"The night he disappeared?"

His eyes register shock, and I see the question forming on his lips.

"Yes," I say. "I have seen Gabe, and he told me what happened. But he's vanished again, and I'm scared. Scared for him and—and others. Others like Benny."

The priest wrestles for his next words, but I turn away—not in the direction of my own house, where I could crawl into familiar and silent corners, but toward the O'Neils'. He sees my resolve to do what I should have done days before.

"Jocelyn, be sensible!" he barks. "Anything you say will hurt Gabe, will hurt his family. And who would believe you anyway?"

I stop. A crow soars overhead, buoyed by nothing more than sky. "I can't help it if they don't believe me. I can't let that possibility stop me."

"Jocelyn!" He reaches out to grab my wrist, but I

step back. I don't know what he sees on my face, but he drops his hand.

"Father Warren," I say, "I'm not sure I believe in the devil. But if I keep quiet, then I'll be in partnership with you." I breathe deeply. "And I couldn't bear that."

I turn and stumble, but I catch myself and continue down the O'Neils' walkway, knowing I will be the first stone thrown—the first rock in the avalanche.

"And you didn't come directly to us?"

"Please, Mike," Margo says.

I shake my head. "I know that I should have."

"Damn right you should have." Mike's face is red, his eyes huge. "Do you have any idea what this has been like for us?"

"Jocelyn. Tell us again, about Gabe's state of mind," says Margo, leaning toward me. "What did he look like? Was he distraught? Do you think he'd do anything drastic?"

"I don't know." I'm gulping for air. I've betrayed Gabe. I've added to his parents' suffering. I may be the cause of—

"When I get my hands on Warren, he'll wish he'd never been born."

"We have to find Gabe," says Margo. "We have to call the police."

"Jesus," says Mike, cringing. "And what good would that do?"

"They can help us find him. We have new information. Please, Mike."

"It would only make matters worse for Gabe. Don't you see that? He could never come home."

"But, Mike . . . ," says Margo, reaching her hand out to him.

He shrugs her off. "I'm calling the bishop," he says. "That's the first step."

"Jocelyn," says Margo. Tears are running down her face. "Would you go get your mother for me? Please?"

"Jocelyn." Mike's voice stops me. "You are not to say one word to anyone. You know nothing about Gabe. Do you understand me?"

I'm paralyzed.

"The boy you describe is not my son. Not my son."

Mom runs to be with Margo. I don't know what to do. I pick up the phone and call Benny.

"Can you come get me?" I ask.

"Right now?"

"Sooner."

I tell Benny that I've seen Gabe, that he may still be in town. We drive around searching for him. We get out and look under the railroad bridge. We climb up to the top of the bridge, and then we walk the railway.

I call out Gabe's name, thinking he might be hiding in the bushes, waiting. Benny walks behind me. I don't want Gabe to know that anyone is with me.

I think about Gabe being somewhere out there, alone. Alone? I walk back toward Benny and say, "Let's go check the parish house."

Benny gives me a puzzled look, but so far my urgency has prevented him from asking too many questions. We pull up in front.

Benny turns off the headlights, and there is Father Warren coming out of the house, suitcase in hand.

"Is he meeting Gabe?" asks Benny. Insight flashes over his face.

"I don't know," I say. "Maybe."

Another priest steps out of the driver's side of a black car parked in front of us. He takes the suitcase from Father Warren and puts it in the trunk.

"I guess not," I say.

"You want to tell me what's going on?" asks Benny.

I look down at my hands. Where to start? "Benny," I say.

Benny studies my face.

"Has Father Warren . . ." I look up. "Has he ever come on—"

"Oh," he says. "Has he been trying to get in my pants?"

I nod.

"It's occurred to me, yes."

I'm measuring how much is right for me to share.

Benny says, "I guess it occurred to Gabe, too."

I nod my head. "Why didn't you tell me?"

"I don't know," he says. "I've been so confused about everything. I feel like God's been giving me this massive test and there's no way I can pass."

"Especially when you've been hanging out with cheap girls like me?" I say.

Benny looks out the window. When he turns back, I can see that his eyes are moist. "Every time I was with you, I felt guilty. So guilty, so scared—when Warren wanted to interrogate me, I couldn't say no. I needed to set things right for my mother, but I also needed to keep a safe distance from him."

I reach out and take Benny's hand. "Do you get this?" I say. "Nothing about this summer has been cheap, Benny. Nothing."

The church is full by the time I arrive for the
funeral. I search for a single person whom I
might cling to, but other than the baseball players
who give me awkward smiles as I pass, most of the
solemn people sitting in the pews are strangers. A
woman in front of me stops in the aisle to chat, giving me a moment to scan the faces.

I see Benny's. He waves me to the front where he's
sitting, and I'm overwhelmed by his generosity. "I'm
so glad you're here," he says, kissing my forehead.

"Of course I'm here! My heart is breaking for you,
Benny," I say, holding him tight.

Benny and I haven't seen much of each other this
summer. He decided to stop avoiding his mother's ill-
ness and to stop bartering with God to make her
well. Instead, he stayed close by reading her books,
helping her to write letters. She died two days ago,

on a brilliant blue August day, with Benny and his father at her side.

That's not to say that Benny and I haven't continued talking. We have. Mostly late at night by phone—it's easier that way. It's been good to realize that even when I can't see my reflection in Benny's eyes, I still exist.

A moment later my own mother slides into the pew next to me. She smiles at Benny and his father and then takes my hand in hers. "I didn't know you were coming," I say.

"I thought you might need me." She looks forward, implying that says it all.

The organ plays, and the young replacement priest proceeds down the aisle behind the cross. I look at him and whisper a thank-you to God for the hundredth time.

And I think of Gabe. How can I help it? I slip my hand into my skirt pocket and feel the tattered edges of his envelope—postmarked from Jacksonville, Florida. Inside is a single scratch-and-win ticket. That's it. Just a ticket. I showed the envelope to Margo, and she hugged me until my shirt was soaked from tears. "He's alive," she said like a prayer. I wish Gabe had sent his mom a ticket. Or maybe he did—trusting that I would bring it to her. I haven't scratched the ticket's silver circles to see what lies beneath. Sometime maybe.

A gust of warm air flows into the church. Mrs. Desanctis would have liked this summer day, I think. The odor of incense mingles with flowers and burning candles. I listen to the sounds of chants, of bells, of prayers in song. When the priest holds the host high in the air and then bends to kiss the altar, I grasp the cross at my neck. I remember the day that Margo gave it to me. How I believed in the magic that would transform me from an ordinary girl into something sacred.

The service is nearly over when the sun suddenly rises over the mountains and beams shine through the stained-glass windows. Rays of reds, oranges, and blues scatter across the congregation.

I look down at myself, stained by color. No. Not stained. Celebrated. And it occurs to me that perhaps souls are like prisms. Prisms that allow us to see clearly into the soul of another and, at the same time, recognize our own glorious light.